AGENT

UNDERCOVER

PROTECTORS

UNDERCOVER

BOOK ONE

USA TODAY BESTSELLING AUTHOR

HEATHER SLADE

ISBN: 979-8-88649-095-4

MORE FROM AUTHOR HEATHER SLADE

BUTLER RANCH
Kade's Worth
Brodie's Promise
Maddox's Truce
Naughton's Secret
Mercer's Vow
Kade's Return
Butler Ranch Christmas

WICKED WINEMAKERS
FIRST LABEL
Brix's Bid
Ridge's Release
Press' Passion
Zin's Sins
Tryst's Temptation

WICKED WINEMAKERS
SECOND LABEL
Beau's Beloved
Coming Soon:
Cru's Crush
Bones' Bliss
Snapper's Seduction
Kick's Kiss

ROARING FORK RANCH
Coming Soon:
Roaring Fork Wrangler
Roaring Fork Roughstock
Roaring Fork Rockstar
Roaring Fork Rooker
Roaring Fork Bridger

THE ROYAL AGENTS
OF MI6
Make Me Shiver
Drive Me Wilder
Feel My Pinch
Chase My Shadow
Find My Angel

K19 SECURITY
SOLUTIONS TEAM ONE
Razor's Edge
Gunner's Redemption
Mistletoe's Magic
Mantis' Desire
Dutch's Salvation

K19 SECURITY
SOLUTIONS TEAM TWO
Striker's Choice
Monk's Fire
Halo's Oath
Tackle's Honor
Onyx's Awakening

K19 SHADOW OPERATIONS
TEAM ONE
Code Name: Ranger
Code Name: Diesel
Code Name: Wasp
Code Name: Cowboy
Code Name: Mayhem

K19 ALLIED INTELLIGENCE
TEAM ONE
Code Name: Ares
Code Name: Cayman
Code Name: Poseidon
Coming soon:
Code Name: Zeppelin
Code Name: Magnet

K19 ALLIED INTELLIGENCE
TEAM TWO
Coming Soon:
Code Name: Michelangelo
Code Name: Typhon
Code Name: Hornet
Code Name: Reaper
Code Name: Rogue

PROTECTORS
UNDERCOVER
Undercover Agent
Coming Soon:
Undercover Savior
Undercover Prince
Undercover Infidel
Undercover Assassin

THE INVINCIBLES
TEAM ONE
Decked
Edged
Grinded
Riled
Smoked

THE INVINCIBLES
TEAM TWO
Bucked
Irished
Sainted
Hammered
Ripped

THE UNSTOPPABLES
TEAM ONE
Furied
Merried

COWBOYS OF
CRESTED BUTTE
A Cowboy Falls
A Cowboy's Dance
A Cowboy's Kiss
A Cowboy Stays
A Cowboy Wins

Table of Contents

1

Emerson

There was something about a man with a British accent that melted my panties. That it was a hundred degrees with the same amount of humidity, melted the rest of me. The Englishman who said good morning and held the door open as I walked out of my air-conditioned building and he walked in, didn't seem affected by the scorching temps in the slightest.

"Can I help you find something?" I asked when I saw the man stop at the bank of mailboxes. Maybe letting a stranger saunter into the building just because of his nothing-to-do-with-the-weather hotness hadn't been the smartest thing to do.

"I'm a friend of Niven's," he said, not looking at me but peering through the tiny window of the jam-packed box instead.

"Oh, Tommy? Of course, that makes sense."

He turned to me and cocked his head, but immediately focused his attention back on the mailbox.

"I haven't seen him for several days." Hence the overflowing mail. It wasn't unusual, though. The man who lived at the opposite end of the hall from me was out of town more than he was in. The part that made sense was that Tommy, as I called him, was British too. "Was he expecting you?" I asked as if it were any of my business. Anything, though, to have a reason to keep staring at the man who reminded me of Pierce Brosnan's James Bond—the *Golden Eye* version.

My penchant for movies made the same year I was born or earlier, meant that most of the men who turned my head on screen were now in their sixties or seventies. The dark-haired hottie in front of me, the one I was admiring from head to foot—the same man who was speaking to me—was closer to my own age. *The man who was speaking to me.*

"I'm sorry, can you please repeat that?" I asked while, at the same time, trying to figure out why he looked so familiar—the sunglasses and baseball cap he wore didn't make it easy.

"I said I wasn't certain of my date of arrival."

As much as I didn't want to take my eyes off Mister 007, I glanced at my phone. "Oh! I need to go!" I exclaimed, dismayed to see that if I didn't leave now, I wouldn't have a prayer of arriving at work in time for my nine o'clock meeting. "Sorry. Maybe I'll see you around."

The man nodded, but didn't appear to have heard me; James Bond would never have been so rude.

Hoisting one of the three canvas bags I was carrying onto my shoulder, I rushed out of the building just in time to see the number one bus pull away from my corner stop. "Dammit," I muttered under my breath. What would've taken me twelve minutes would now be forty-two; the next bus wouldn't come for a half hour.

I turned at the exact, right moment to see the man formerly—albeit momentarily—known as my own British superspy leave the building and walk in the opposite direction. I leaned against the lamppost, inwardly swooning at the way his steel-hard ass looked in his trousers, as Tommy would call them. His shoulders were ridiculously broad, and even though he wore a long-sleeve dress shirt, I could see his muscular arms as he moved. *But that ass.* I could barely bring myself to look away.

Tommy. When had I last seen him? It had to have been at least two weeks. I crossed my fingers that the other Brit's arrival meant he was back in town. Things ended so awkwardly between us the last time I saw him, and before I had the chance to talk to him about it, he was gone again.

I touched my lips with my fingers, remembering the kiss he and I had shared that night. It had been so unexpected. We'd gone out for dinner several times, but until that moment, it hadn't occurred to me that Tommy was interested in me. Maybe it was just that I was so out of practice, I missed the signs.

I sighed. My dating slump had lasted longer than I cared to acknowledge even to myself. I was a self-proclaimed nerd, burying myself in global-political grand strategy to the point of exclusion of everything else in my life. Dating—who had the time? Fashion—why bother when the only people who ever saw me were other analysts who also had their noses buried in foreign-policy documents?

My last long-term boyfriend had been a professor, also in the international program, but on the Russian side. We broke up the day I walked into his office to find his associate on her back on his desk, legs spread, skirt around her waist, and panties on the floor, beside him.

It had definitely put me off Eastern European men, but Brits? They were my weakness. Ever since the one night when I decided to act the role of someone far different than who I usually am—someone adventurous, worldly, passionate, and wanton.

I shook my head against the memory. Thinking about the best sex I'd ever had wouldn't help the ache of not having any in so long get better.

I set my bags down on the sidewalk and rolled my shoulders. I had a long day ahead of me, and starting out thirty minutes late wasn't going to make it any shorter.

I checked the time on my phone again, and given it hadn't stood still for me, I contemplated whether it would be better to call a car service and be on time, or my assistant, Paxon Warrick, to tell him I'd be late for the third time this week. Since it was only Wednesday, the car service was probably the best bet, especially considering we had an important meeting scheduled in forty-five minutes.

"Everything okay?" said an English-accented voice from behind me. When I spun around and looked into my friend's friend's green eyes, he was elevated right back to superspy status.

Oh my God—those green eyes. I'd never forget them. It had been three years since I last saw them and the man standing in front of me. I wanted to look him up and down, but I wasn't wearing sunglasses to hide my once-over. *Keep your eyes up here*, I told myself, focusing on his face.

"I missed my bus. Do you wear contacts?"

He shook his head, cocking it to the side like he had when I mentioned Tommy. "What an odd question."

"Your eyes. They're the color of sage after it rains. Not grayish like Dusty Miller."

Now he looked perplexed. "Who is Dusty Miller?"

"Not who. What. It's a plant."

If anything, my explanation left him looking more puzzled. The fact that we were in the midst of our second conversation and he showed no sign of recognizing me, didn't come as a surprise. I looked nothing like I had that night.

Gone were the sophisticated clothes I'd purchased for my first-ever international policy conference in London and then never wore again. In their place, I had on a sensible, wrinkle-resistant black pantsuit, a short-sleeve white blouse, and comfortable black pumps with a one-inch heel. Instead of the contacts I'd had in when I last saw this man, I was wearing my round, tortoise-shell glasses that caused less eyestrain when I spent hours upon hours reading. And, like most days, my hair was bone straight instead of falling down my back in soft waves as it had that night.

The other thing—while the man in front of me had been my sole indiscretion, the only one-night stand I'd had in my life, there was no doubt that I was one of countless for him.

A car pulled up at the curb beside us. "Can I give you a lift somewhere?"

Could I sit in such close proximity to him when he had no recollection of how he'd rocked my world one night three years ago? "No, I'll just wait for the next bus, but thank you."

He studied me as though that response confused him as much as my referring to his eyes as the color of a plant. "Where are you going?"

"MIT." I pointed down Mass Ave. "You know, in Cambridge."

"I do know. I'm going there myself."

"Really?"

"I'd hardly lie about it."

I looked at the time on my phone again. It was speeding by, and I was going to be late if I didn't accept his offer of a ride, and that would be even if I called for my own car service.

"If you're sure it wouldn't be an imposition."

"It wouldn't."

His voice, the one that had played over and over again in my head in the months that followed our sexcapades, didn't sound anything like what I remembered.

Instead of being suave and sexy, he was clipped and curt. I remembered him being cocky, not rude.

He opened the door and picked up all three of my bags, motioning for me to get in. Before I could scoot to the far side of the back-passenger seat, he closed the door and walked around to the other side.

"Sir," the man behind the wheel said when my Mister One-Nighter got in. Before my backseat companion could tell him where we were going, the driver sped off.

On the best of days, like Sundays at four in the morning, it took me seven minutes to get from my apartment to my office. Today I'd be there in under five at the rate the man otherwise employed as a Nascar driver was going. The last time I'd felt this carsick was on Mister Toad's Wild Ride at Disneyland.

"You can drop me at this corner," I said when the driver pulled up at the intersection of Memorial and Wadsworth. "Thank you for the ride." I realized then that he hadn't introduced himself, and neither had I. However, I had been preoccupied with me remembering him and him not remembering me—along with not hurling my breakfast on the floor of the car.

I turned to shake his hand and thank him properly, but he'd already climbed out the other side of the car and was holding my three bags.

"I'm Emme," I said when he opened my door and I got out of the car.

"Lennox," he answered.

Hmm. Lennox? Not Lynx as he'd introduced himself that night? *Interesting.*

"Shall we?" he asked so abruptly that it pushed my annoyance over the edge.

"It was nice to meet you, although you look very familiar to me. Like maybe we've met before." I gave him time to acknowledge having the same recollection I had. When he didn't, I prompted him further. "Do I look at all familiar to you?"

Still no response. Wait. What was he doing? When I turned around, I caught him looking at himself in the window of my building. How could he possibly remember me when he was so busy admiring his own reflection?

God, what did I expect? Hadn't I just reminded myself that I was probably only one on a miles-and-miles-long list of one-night conquests for the man I'd met in a hotel bar? I should be happy he didn't recognize me.

When I walked away, he followed, reminding me he still had my bags. "This is my building." I held out my hands, which he ignored.

"Mine as well."

"Oh…um…which department?"

"International Policy. I have a meeting with Dr. Charles."

I stopped walking and groaned inwardly. "You're kidding."

His perplexed expression reappeared. "I'm not," he said with a furrowed brow.

"I'm Dr. Charles."

2

Lynx

The lovely creature standing in front of me, the one with big ocean-blue eyes and hair the color of my favorite tawny port, the one I'd recognized the moment I saw her, the one I couldn't walk away from this morning even though I should have…was the woman Saint referred to as Charlie?

Based on his description of her, I'd expected *Charlie* to be someone older, not closer to his age and mine.

I hadn't recognized her in the photographs in her dossier; they certainly hadn't done her remote justice. I had, though, the minute she passed me by when I entered Saint's building. I had no reason to, but I'd hovered at the mailboxes earlier just so my gaze on her could linger.

As she studied something on her mobile, I studied her. It had been three years since I last saw Emerson. At the time, she hadn't referred to herself as Emme, and I hadn't known her last name.

I didn't remember her being as thin as she was. She looked like a runner based on the leanness of her arms and legs. I also didn't recall her tits being smaller than average, but that didn't stop them from registering with my cock.

She raised her head, scrunching her eyes. "My meeting is with Adam Benjamin. You are not Dr. Benjamin."

"He had a last-minute emergency. I'm here on his behalf."

"Oh. That's odd. How do you know Tommy?"

I smiled at the way she jumped between topics in a single sentence. "That's the second time you referred to 'Tommy.' Are you speaking of Niven St. Thomas?"

"Right. Sorry. I call him Tommy; he calls me Charlie."

I shook my head. Saint hadn't mentioned her nickname for him; only his for her. The other thing Saint had told me, which now made my blood pressure skyrocket, was that he and Dr. Charles had been seeing one another. The wanker was the epitome of a womanizing rake. I'd never known Saint to spend more than a single night with any one woman. Not that I'd spent more than that single night with this one either.

She slid her mobile into her handbag and rested one hand on her hip. "Are you aware that Dr. Benjamin and I were meeting about…" she leaned in closer and looked left and right. "China?"

I repeated her motions. "Yes. I am."

"How did you say you know Tom—Mr. St. Thomas?"

Still leaning close to her, I breathed in her scent. The memory of the one night we spent together roared through my mind. I wasn't typically a fan of perfume of any kind, but I remembered hers being enticing.

"I didn't," I murmured, closing my eyes to sort the different fragrances in my head. She smelled of bergamot orange, morning jasmine, and evening rose petals, with a hint of vanilla and patchouli mixed in. Its potency made my eyes roll back in my head and my mouth water as I recalled running my tongue over her body, tasting her skin.

When I reopened my eyes, Dr. Charles appeared transfixed. She still stood as close, but her head was angled away from me.

"Are you *smelling* me?" she asked.

Caught, I smiled. "Your perfume is beguiling," I said without apology.

"I don't wear perfume," she responded, grabbing my arm with the hand previously on her hip and leading me to the building's entrance. She swiped a card in the slot by the door and then rested her palm on the dark-gray square beneath it. "Sorry, protocol," she said, slipping inside the door and closing it behind her.

I was well aware of the security measures in place at MIT. Given the nature of the work done within this building's walls, security was as tight here as it was at Vauxhall Cross. After repeating the same security process she had completed, I joined her inside.

"I admit to being intrigued by your association with my friend, I mean neighbor." She squared her shoulders. "My neighbor friend, Mister…"

Flustered, Emerson's cheeks turned the most delightful shade of pink.

"Please call me Lennox."

She closed one eye and pointed her index finger at me with her thumb raised, mimicking a gun, and then brought her hand forward and poked my upper arm. "Again, you dodged my question." She walked into the lift as though she didn't anticipate I would follow.

When we exited on the eighth floor, a man I knew but had to pretend I didn't, was waiting.

"Good morning, Emme," he said before turning to me. "This must be Mr. Edgemon. I'm Paxon Warrick." He held out his hand, and I shook it.

"Emerson," I murmured, loving that name so much more than the nickname the man known to me as Irish had just used.

"Yes?" she asked with wide eyes and a furrowed brow.

"Do you need a few moments before our meeting?"

"Um…sure," she answered. "How did you know my…never mind. I'm sure it was in Dr. Benjamin's notes."

I nodded, waiting to see if my slip let on I'd recognized her like I guessed she had me.

"I'll show our guest to the conference room," Irish offered.

"Wait. Were you aware we were meeting with Mr. Edgemon instead of Dr. Benjamin?"

"I was."

As I watched her face go from puzzled to pensive, I wondered why Irish wasn't handling this better.

"I received an email. I assumed you did too," he said, but it seemed too little, too late.

"Hmm," she murmured, picking up her bags. "I'll just be a moment." She walked away, leaving me alone with the undercover agent the CIA had put in place when MI6 brought Saint in.

"Follow me," he said when she disappeared down the hallway. "Coffee? No, wait. You're a tea drinker."

"Neither, thanks. Water would be nice, though."

Irish led me into what looked like more of a war room than a place to meet. "I'll forewarn you that Emme—Dr. Charles—can be…quirky, and that's an understatement. But she's a brilliant analyst."

"As well as strategist." And so much more than that. She was the woman I'd never been able to forget, and the one I never thought I'd see again.

Irish murmured his agreement, grabbed an envelope from the other side of the table, and slid it in front of me. "Beautiful too."

Him saying so set me on edge, just like it had remembering that Saint told me they'd been seeing each other. "How close are the two of you?"

"Not as close as I'd like, but after this mission is over, who knows?"

My jaw tightened. Not if I had anything to say about it. And I planned to. Irish was out of his league. Way out. If I wanted Emerson—and I did—I'd have her. He and Saint could both be damned.

"She hasn't let on that she knows anything about Saint's disappearance," he said quietly when he returned with my glass of water. "Or Dr. Benjamin's," he added as an afterthought.

"That was evident."

"How so?"

"We crossed paths at their apartment building."

"What did she say?"

I explained that I'd encountered *Emme* exiting Saint's building earlier as I was going in. "There wasn't anything specific, only that her demeanor when I mentioned knowing Niven was one of curiosity rather than concern."

"Serendipitous, meeting her," he commented.

"Or not." I would've preferred to keep my association with Saint a secret longer than I had.

"Have a seat." Irish motioned to a chair.

"I'll wait for Dr. Charles. In fact, I'd prefer to meet with her alone."

"Why?"

I was beginning to think a talk with Irish's boss was in order. In the hierarchy of either of our agencies, I was several ranks above the man. I raised a brow.

"She expects me to be in the meeting."

"I'm sure you'll think of something."

He appeared annoyed, but that wasn't my problem.

"Let me know when you'd like to debrief," he said before he walked out of the room.

A few minutes later, Emerson joined me. "I apologize about Mr. Warrick…Paxon…my assistant. Apparently, he had another appointment."

"As he mentioned."

"Oh. Huh. Well…shall we get started?" she asked without preamble of further small talk, which I found surprisingly disappointing. I usually abhorred mindless chatter, but in this case, I wanted to hear more of the beautiful lilt to her voice.

Her scent wafted in the air, and the desirability the woman exuded made my ability to keep my head on business nearly impossible. I adjusted my trousers and took a seat where she indicated I should.

"After his last visit, Dr. Benjamin sent over key points he wanted to cover when he returned." As she reached around me to pick up the envelope that Irish had slid my way, her elbow knocked over the glass of water, the entirety of its contents emptying all over my lap. Simultaneously, the papers contained in the envelope spilled out and scattered on the floor at my feet.

"Oh, dear, I'm such a klutz," she mumbled, dropping to her knees in front of me to clean up the mess before I could stand to do the same. As it was, she was between my legs, head slightly bowed.

Without stepping over her, I was powerless to do anything to help. "Emerson?"

"Yes?" When she looked up, it was obvious she realized where, exactly, her head was in correlation to my cock. Her cheeks flushed, and she tried to scoot away, only to bang into the chair behind her. When she grasped it in an attempt to stand and it slid away, I watched as her head smacked into the table before I could prevent it from happening.

"Fuck, that hurt," she muttered, pushing the offending chair back, landing on her bottom, and rubbing her head.

I stood and held my hand out to help her do the same. When she grasped it with hers, we both noticed blood on her fingers.

"Stay where you are and let me take a look."

"That's okay, I can—"

"I said, stay where you are." Putting my hand on her shoulder, I held her in place; I could see dark red blood seeping into her lighter red hair. "You've got a laceration. Stitches will likely be necessary."

"I'll be fine," she snapped, swatting my hand away. "And you're kind of bossy." Refusing to look me in the eye, she grabbed the offending table's edge and pulled herself up.

"Take this and press it to your scalp," I told her, placing my handkerchief in her palm and then guiding her hand to where she was bleeding.

I saw her start to sway and caught her before she toppled over. She was facing me, her free hand on my arm.

I told myself I was looking into her eyes for signs of a concussion, but the truth was, I was mesmerized by the swirling shades of ocean blue. Her pupils were dilated, but when my gaze drifted lower, the hardened nipples I could see through her thin blouse indicated her visceral reaction was more likely caused by our close proximity than the bump on her head. My cock was certainly reacting in a way I had little control of.

Was she remembering the same thing I was? How we'd spent one night having the best sex I'd had in my life? And that was saying something. While the pretty redhead wasn't the most experienced lover I'd ever been with, there was something about her, about the way our bodies came together, like two perfect circles entwined, that I'd never been able to forget.

"You can let go now," she murmured, taking her hand off my arm.

Reluctantly, I did as she asked, and she took a step toward the door.

"Where are you going?"

"Um, my office. I have some…first aid supplies."

"I'll go with you." I held my arm out, but she didn't take it, so instead, I kept my hand on the small of her back.

She peeked over her shoulder. "I'm fine," she repeated.

I wasn't certain she would be once she saw the amount of blood that had seeped into her hair and my handkerchief. Head wounds tended to bleed a lot, but at the rate hers was, she had no choice but to see a physician to get it closed up.

"Wait here," I said, eyeing a roll of paper towels on the counter in what looked like a small kitchen. Grabbing a few in one hand, I gently removed the blood-soaked cloth and then folded another few into a square. I took her right hand and brought it up to hold it in place. "You really need to see a physician," I said again.

"Right," she murmured, continuing down the hallway into an office that I would have immediately known was hers, even without her in it. I couldn't pinpoint exactly why; it was just a feeling I got when I crossed the threshold.

"Sorry for the mess, I'm…reorganizing," she muttered as she opened a desk drawer and pointed to a large red case with a white cross on the top. "Could you please help me with this?"

"Of course." The box looked big enough to supply a mobile critical care unit and as though it weighed a metric ton. I hoisted it onto the desk. "Are you the paramedic on staff for all of MIT?"

Ignoring my remark, she opened the lid and rummaged through the contents. Evidently, the first aid kit was also slated for reorganization.

"Here it is," she said, pulling a smaller box from the case. "Would you mind?" she asked, handing it to me.

I stared at her, incredulous. "What am I doing with that?"

Emerson pulled out a small vial and stopper. "It's a liquid bandage. It should work fine."

"Are you suggesting that I put this on your laceration as opposed to seeking medical attention?"

"Never mind," she said, grabbing the items from my hand and stalking out of her office. Once again, I was on her heels.

"You can either wait in my office, or we can reschedule for another time," she said when she realized I was behind her.

"No," I said at the same time Irish walked into the lobby from the other direction.

"What happened?" He gasped with a horrified expression when he saw the bloody towels Emerson held to her head. Then, his gaze landed on my drenched trousers.

"A little accident. I spilled water, and then things just got…worse," she said, trying to get around him.

When he grabbed her arm and led her over to a chair in the lobby, it was all I could do not to throttle him.

"Sit there and don't move," he barked and then turned to me. "She has a first aid kit in her office."

"Yes," I said, pointing to the vial of liquid she held tight in her hand.

"What's that?" he asked, looking from me to her.

"It's a liquid bandage. If you'd just put some on my cut, it will stop the bleeding."

"Is she kidding?"

"I'm afraid she's somewhat intransigent." While my irritation with the undercover agent posing as her assistant was reaching an epic proportion, I found Emerson's stubbornness absolutely adorable.

"Let me have a look." Irish moved her hand and lifted the sopping paper towels. "It's bleeding a lot and looks to be about five centimeters. I'm sorry, Emme, but you're going to have to go to the emergency room."

"No!" she shrieked, startling us both. "No hospitals."

I nudged Irish out of the way and knelt in front of her. I put my hand on her knee, but what I really wanted to do was scoop her into my arms.

"The laceration is this long," I said, holding my thumb and index finger apart. "Your desired treatment won't stop the bleeding. You need to see a doctor."

Emerson's eyes bored into mine as though she was pleading with me to understand, and I did, or at least, I thought I did. It wasn't about seeing a doctor; there was something about going to a hospital that set her off.

"Medical services is closed until two," Irish said, looking at his watch. "What about Cambridge Urgent Care?"

Emerson's eyes opened wide like they had when he mentioned the emergency room.

"I've another idea. Give me a moment?"

She nodded.

I stepped several paces away, pulled out my mobile, and sent a text. Moments later, the device rang.

"Lennox, how are you? Have you arrived in Boston?"

"I'm well, Stephen, thanks. I'm in Cambridge."

"As am I. I'm attending a conference at MIT." I knew he was. "We're on a break presently."

"How much longer is your break?"

"Let's see…another fifteen minutes."

"Where are you specifically?"

"Building 14—"

"One moment," I said to Stephen. "Emerson, where is building 14?"

Irish answered for her, pointing. "Right behind that building there."

"Is it where the medical services are located?"

"Yes, but—"

I held up my hand and raised the mobile to my ear. "Wait there. I need you to take a look at a head injury."

3

Emerson

"What's going on?" I asked when *Lennox* put his phone in his pocket and walked back over to where Paxon held a fresh set of paper towels against my head.

He knelt in front of me like he had a few minutes earlier, and my heart rate increased tenfold—as it had right after I humiliated myself by spilling water on him. I studied him studying me. How was it possible that he didn't recognize me after staring into my eyes like he was?

"My cousin Stephen is a physician, who happens to be here at MIT for a medical conference. Will you allow him to take a look at your cut?"

I was almost disappointed that he didn't say laceration again. It flowed so smoothly off his English-accented tongue in that swoon-worthy James Bondy way. This was the voice I remembered, not the one he'd used earlier that made me feel like a forgettable nuisance.

"Yes," I said when I realized he was waiting for an answer.

"Will you be okay?" Paxon squeezed my shoulder.

"I'll be with her," Lynx snapped at him.

"Right. Well, I'll be in the office later if you need anything."

"I need to get my purse…and my phone." I rushed away from the two men in the lobby, who oddly, appeared as though they were about to come to blows, and went to my office to grab my things. When I looked up from my desk, Lynx stood in the doorway, just as handsome as I remembered.

He had to be well over six feet, with hair so dark it almost looked black. His green eyes were piercing as they stared into mine. I let my gaze drift down the length of him. He wore a pale blue dress shirt with black trousers and brown wingtips. The way his clothes fit his body, I doubted he was any less fit than he had been three years ago. Even without closing my eyes— which I refused to allow myself to do—I could feel his powerful arms around me and the way his steely pecs and abs felt when I ran my hands over them.

"Ahem." Did his lip twitch right before he cleared his throat, startling me out of admiring him? "Ready?" he asked, with a full smirk now on display.

I nodded and swept past him, beyond irritated that he saw me doing what so many other women obviously did.

He caught up and kept his hand on the small of my back as he led me over to the elevator. His fingertips alone sent an electrical current straight through my body. When it settled between my legs, I shuddered.

The door to the elevator opened, and I couldn't say whether I was relieved or troubled that it was empty. Standing less than a foot from me was the only man I'd ever let myself get so carried away with that it didn't matter we'd just met in the bar of the hotel where my conference was being held. My attraction to him was immediate, then and now. Our bodies spoke to one another that night as though we were already lov-ers. That he had no recollection of me, nearly broke my heart.

The elevator dinged again, and we stepped out into the lobby. Before we exited the building, he took my hand in his. What I should find comforting, only increased my irritation.

"This way," I said when we walked past the build-ing across from mine. As we rounded the corner, a man standing in front of the medical services building raised his hand; Lynx did the same.

"What happened to you?" the man smirked and asked when we got closer.

"Spilled-water incident, which resulted in Dr. Charles hitting her head quite hard."

"Come with me. I made arrangements for someone to open the clinic," the man said.

He was as gorgeous and captivating as Lynx, but in an entirely different way. Where Lynx was a high-handed, arrogant, no-nonsense know-it-all, his cousin…doctor…doctor-cousin…had a glint in his eye that gave me the impression that under different circumstances, he might be a mischievous tease.

We followed him inside, past the unmanned check-in desk, and into an exam room. "Let's have a look, shall we?"

I let go of the paper towels that I was holding against the cut. As soon as I did, Lynx took them and threw them in the waste can; the other man donned gloves.

"I'm Stephen," he said as he parted my hair and took a look. "I'm Lennox's cousin as well as a doctor."

"Emerson," I said, cringing when his fingers touched my scalp. "Nice to meet you."

"You don't have to fib. You won't hurt my feelings considering I'm hurting you far more. I should've asked before, but any allergies? To latex, for example?"

"No. None."

"Good. I wouldn't want you breaking out in a wretched rash on top of bleeding profusely from the nasty gash in your head." He winked and leaned closer to me. "Tell me, did my evil cousin do this to you? I seem to remember an incident where Lennox convinced me to get on our grandfather's Penny-farthing, which I promptly fell from. That was a right mess." The entire time he chattered, he pressed a gauze pad filled with antiseptic on and around the cut.

"I did nothing of the kind."

As opposed to Lynx's scowl, Stephen's smile was infectious. He tossed the gauze into the garbage, took off his gloves, and turned around to face me. "The laceration on your scalp is ghastly, but I assure you, you won't bleed to death. I do need to close it up."

"Okay," I murmured when he appeared to be waiting for an answer from me.

"Be right back," he said to me and then turned to Lynx. "Try not to do anything to further injure my patient in my absence."

Lynx rolled his eyes and stood in front of me when we were alone.

"How are you feeling?"

"Embarrassed."

He smiled. "Are you dizzy? Feeling nauseous?"

I was, but I doubted either had to do with me cutting my head. He made me dizzy—lust-filled vertigo. And the nausea? That related to how humiliated I was both by my over-the-top clumsiness and the fact he had no recollection that we spent an entire night naked in one another's arms.

"Have you had staples before?" Stephen asked when he returned.

"No, but they sound painful."

"I won't lie. They are. But for a scalp wound, they're the best option, given how thick the skin is. I'd offer to numb the area first, but to be honest, the lidocaine hurts worse than the staples do." He motioned to Lynx, who took my hand.

"Here we go," said Stephen. "Try not to move."

"*Ouch!*" I shouted, but by the time I did, he was finished.

"All set. Those will stay in for a few days, and then they'll need to be removed by a doctor." Stephen looked down at where Lynx still had a firm hold on my hand and then back up at me. I tried to get him to let go, which only resulted in him holding on tighter.

"You may be mildly concussed. Do you have someone to look after you?"

"I will," Lynx announced.

My head snapped in his direction. "That won't be necessary. I can—"

"What needs to be done?" he asked Stephen as though I hadn't said a word. I wrenched my hand from his, intending to protest, but Stephen had already handed Lynx my care instructions and the two were reviewing them.

"Keep an eye for any signs of nausea, dizziness, fever, or if she loses consciousness, bring her here or to an emergency room. Also," he said, looking at me, "you'll likely soon have a dickens of a headache. While at first you may suppose it's from my cousin's incessant chatter, as hard as it might be to believe, it'll be caused more by your injury. Please forgive me in advance for what I'm about to say, but you shouldn't be left alone for the next twenty-four hours."

His smirk made me smile.

He turned back to Lynx, who I caught rolling his eyes for the second time. I could imagine these two as young boys. Stephen forever the tease. Lynx spoiling his fun.

The reality of what he'd said, suddenly dawned on me. There was no way I could spend another minute with Lynx, let alone hours. "My parents live in the city. I'll just go to their place."

"What else?" Lynx asked, not acknowledging I'd said a word.

"She needs to rest and avoid caffeine and alcohol. No screen time, and that includes a computer, telly, smart phone, or tablet of any kind. No bright lights or loud noises, and no demanding physical activities." He said the last part directly to me, with a wink.

"What about for the headache?" Lynx asked.

Did he not remember I was still in the room and that even if I did have a concussion, which I doubted, I could see and hear perfectly fine?

"I can prescribe a pain reliever—"

"That won't be necessary," I said, loud enough that both of them turned and looked at me. "Why do doctors insist on prescribing narcotics when an over-the-counter pain reliever would work just fine?"

"Understood," said Stephen. "Any issue with acetaminophen?"

I shook my head, feeling like a bitch for snapping at him the way I had. The man was doing me a favor, after all. Perhaps sensing it, he squeezed my shoulder.

"Staying hydrated will help with that too. And be sure to eat. Nothing too heavy. Okay?"

"Okay," I said, nodding.

He looked at his watch and turned to Lynx. "Sorry to have to run. I'll ring you when I get another break. We'll make plans."

Lynx thanked him, and the two men embraced before Stephen said goodbye to me and left.

"I appreciate you contacting your cousin. As I said, my parents live in Boston. I'll give them a call, and they'll pick me up."

"I'll stay with you until they arrive." He didn't even look up at me. He was studying what looked like my care instructions.

"May I see those?" I snapped—which I seemed to be doing a lot of, but it was *my* damn head injury.

"Of course," he murmured, sheepishly handing them to me.

When I stood and walked out of the clinic, he followed.

"Thank you again," I said once we were outside. "I'll just go to my office and call my mom. Oh, and I'll have Mr. Warrick contact you later about rescheduling. In fact, it might be best for us to wait for Dr. Benjamin to return before continuing. Goodbye." I held out my hand to shake his.

"No."

"Excuse me?" I dropped my arm when he ignored it.

"No, I'm not letting you return to your office alone. No, I'm not going to reschedule with Mr. Warrick. And no, we will not be waiting until Dr. Benjamin returns. As far as you're concerned, I intend to make sure you stick to everything Stephen said."

*The arrogant prick...*I was getting tired of him railroading me. He didn't even remember fucking me, for God's sake. "Who do you think you are? Nothing about me is your business or your responsibility."

He held up one finger, pulled out his cell, and placed a call. "Meet us," he looked up at the street signs. "At the corner of Congress and Memorial."

"*Hey, wait a minute!* I said I would call my parents."

"I have a driver on standby. It's easier."

I stood with my hands on my hips and stared at him. "What?"

"I *said* I would call my parents."

"And I *said* I had a driver on standby. I don't understand what the issue is, Emerson."

I dropped my hands and clenched my fists. This was why a person should never accidentally run into their one-night stand. Just because two people had spent time together naked, didn't mean they knew each other. "The *issue* is that you continue to ignore everything I say."

"You're behaving childishly."

I growled. Literally growled. *"Childishly?* In what way?" I hated the way he was looking at me.

"First, with your insistence that a self-applied liquid bandage would be a sufficient way to stop your laceration from bleeding. Then, your refusal to visit an emergency room. And now, with your unwillingness to accept that you cannot be alone when you have a concussion."

"*Might* have a concussion."

"Another example of childishness."

When he reached out for my hand, I yanked it away.

"Emerson," he growled back at me, sounding enough like my father that it freaked me out. "My driver has arrived. Let's go." He put his hand on my elbow.

"I'm not going anywhere with you and especially not in *that* car with *that* driver."

"Why not?"

"Because riding with Mario Andretti made me nauseous before I had a maybe-concussion."

The look on his face softened, and he gazed into my eyes. "I'll advise him to drive more slowly. Now, please, let me take you home."

He was absolutely, insanely, ridiculously handsome, and when he talked to me in his nice tone of voice, I couldn't resist him, just like I hadn't been able to the night I met him in that bar.

4

Emerson
Three years ago

While the rest of the people I knew attending the London conference had gone out for dinner, I was too jet-lagged to join them. What I really wanted was a glass of wine and something to eat. Then, I planned to take a long, hot soak in the claw-foot tub I saw earlier when I dropped my bags in the room. As tempting as it had been then, I had to hurry downstairs to check-in for the morning session that had begun an hour earlier.

"What can I get you?" asked the bartender, who sounded more Australian than British.

"A glass of Shiraz, please."

He winked, opened a bottle, poured a little in a glass, and set it in front of me. "This is one of my favorites," he said, waiting as I swirled and took a sip.

I nodded. "It's very good." He filled my glass with a bigger pour than I expected.

"Enjoy," he said, winking a second time.

As I studied the menu the cute bartender handed me, I heard a man ask if the seat next to me was taken. I turned to respond and found myself staring wide-eyed and open-mouthed speechless. The man was movie-star, leading-man handsome. The lighting in the bar was dim, but I could see enough to turn my brain to mush.

"Will someone be joining you?" he asked with his hand on the seat back of the bar chair.

"I hope you are," I said, finally finding my voice, but blushing when instead of answering with a simple "no," my mouth decided to announce to the world what my brain was thinking.

He smiled, pulled the chair out slightly, and sat. "I'm Lynx," he said, holding out his hand. He looked me up and down without making any attempt to hide he was doing so.

I wiped my sweaty palm on my skirt and took his extended hand. "Emerson," I said, gazing into eyes that looked like they might be green, but it was too dark to know for sure.

"Lynx," said the bartender. "Welcome back, mate. You out on the pull tonight?"

I watched the man sitting next to me as his eyes scrunched and he laughed and shook his head.

"Sorry. Just kidding, you know?"

"What did he say?" I asked when the Aussie left to take another party's order.

"It was crass," my hot bar neighbor said before taking a long sip of the pint the bartender had given him without him needing to order.

I shrugged. "Tell me anyway."

"Essentially, he asked if I was going to get laid tonight."

"Are you?"

"I usually am."

5

Lynx

On our return trip to Boston, Emerson attempted to contact her parents while I pretended to be distracted by something out the window.

I heard the desperation in her voice as she left a message at the end of her calls, and stole a quick glance, afraid she might be close to tears, but instead, she remained steadfastly annoyed by my presence. I rested my hand next to hers, almost close enough to touch.

"If they don't return your call before we reach your building, I'll stay with you until they do."

"I'll be fine," she whispered, studying our hands.

I found myself questioning whether my decision not to divulge that I remembered our night together had been a good one.

I had no choice, though, at least not yet. My reason for being in Boston had less to do with Emerson—the woman I longed to take into my arms and tell how happy I was to see again—than it did with her role at MIT.

Just the idea that Emerson and Dr. Charles were one and the same, had blindsided me. My decision to act as though we hadn't met prior to this morning was off-the-cuff. The longer I continued the charade, the less I saw an outcome in which I could be honest with her. All I knew for certain was I'd vowed that if I ever saw her again, I would do everything I could to get Emerson back in my bed. Now, that was out of the question. I needed her help to find my missing agent as well as a former British diplomat, who had also disappeared.

Dr. Emme Charles appeared on my radar shortly after she'd gone to work for MIT, where her research on Chinese policy and strategy landed her on the watch-list of nearly every international intelligence agency. Why she used Emme professionally rather than Emerson, remained a mystery.

When Saint moved into the apartment down the hall from hers, it wasn't by accident. He'd been tasked, by me, to convert the brilliant Dr. Charles into an MI6 asset. When the CIA got wind of it, they brought Irish in to do the same thing, only instead of him moving into her building, Irish became her research assistant.

Rather than fight over her, I, along with my counterpart at the CIA, agreed there was no reason she couldn't become a shared asset. However, neither Saint nor Irish had been particularly keen on the idea.

While Saint had been the one to facilitate it behind the scenes, I had been the one to arrange the introduction between Dr. Charles and Adam Benjamin, the man she was supposed to meet with this morning. Dr. Benjamin was not only a former British diplomat, but also a world-renowned expert on China and long-time MI6 asset. When he'd learned of the work Emerson was doing, Dr. Benjamin was anxious to reach out, believing that in her, he'd found a comrade in arms.

With him as a policy influencer for the U.K. and her a policy writer for the U.S., they made a formidable team. They were equally impassioned about the threat China posed not just to our two countries, but to the world.

What loomed great in both their minds was the idea that China had become a "systemic rival" to the world's superpowers, one whose economic power and political influence had grown with unprecedented scale and speed. However, Emerson and Dr. Benjamin had their own agendas—even beyond that of their respective countries. Benjamin's, I feared, had resulted in his disappearance and Saint's, since in addition to being responsible for Emerson's recruitment, he was also on Dr. Benjamin's detail.

"Where are you staying?" Emerson asked when the driver pulled up to her building.

"With Niven."

"Is he in town?"

I shook my head.

"I know your friend said I shouldn't be left alone, but I honestly feel fine," she said as we waited for the lift.

"Stephen isn't a friend; he's my cousin. If it weren't imperative you not be left alone, he wouldn't have said it."

"Tommy's—Mr. St. Thomas'—place is just down the hall. I'll walk over if I'm feeling poorly."

"I'm beginning to think you don't like me," I said with a wink as we exited the lift and I watched her rummage through her handbag.

"Oh no!" she gasped, leaning into the wall and resting her forehead against it.

"You're dizzy. Give me your keys."

"I left my bags in my office. I need to go back."

"We can discuss that later. For now, give me your keys so I can let you into your apartment."

"I need my bags," she said, putting one hand on her hip.

I sighed impatiently. "Very well, what is so important that your bags need to be retrieved today?" I'd been meaning to ask what was in them. The three large canvas bags felt as though they contained bricks.

"Everything." She lifted her head as though she was about to knock it against the wall and then thought better of it. Instead, she looked up at me. "I don't have my keys."

All the better as far as I was concerned. I now had every reason to ignore her pleas to be left on her own.

Saint had had a keypad installed in order to get into his apartment—standard for any MI6 agent whether they were undercover or not—and I had the code. Given the position Emerson held at MIT, I was surprised she hadn't done the same, or that Saint hadn't suggested it. I made a mental note to arrange for one of my team to take care of it.

Emerson walked over to the sofa, and I opened the draperies only to close them again when I remembered that Stephen had advised against bright light.

"He was right about the headache," she mumbled, resting her head against the pillow. I watched as her eyes closed and then opened again, almost in slow motion. "I don't like to take painkillers."

I remembered her reaction to Irish's suggestion she go to an emergency room. The two must somehow relate.

I went into the lavatory and found a bottle of the over-the-counter medicine Stephen mentioned and gave her two tablets along with a glass of water.

"Thank you," she said, handing the glass back to me.

I took it to the kitchen and then looked inside Saint's refrigerator and cupboards. Both were empty sans a few bags of tea.

"When did you last eat?"

When she didn't respond, I walked over to the sofa where she'd stretched out. It appeared she was asleep, but hadn't Stephen also said that if she lost consciousness, I should take her to the hospital?

"Emerson," I whispered, sitting beside her on the cushion.

Her eyes opened quickly, but she seemed disoriented. "Lynx?"

"You fell asleep," I said, brushing her hair from her forehead and pretending I didn't notice her use of a name that, thus far, she had no reason to know. "Very quickly, I might add. I'm sorry I woke you. I was concerned that you might have lost consciousness."

"I'm a good sleeper," she said, averting her eyes.

"I asked when you'd last eaten."

"I had breakfast."

I hadn't, and given it was close to noon, I was famished. I looked out the window and saw a corner market on the other side of Boylston. Dare I leave her long enough to go pick up some groceries?

"Where's your mobile?"

"Right there," she said, pointing to the table next to the sofa.

I picked it up, put in my number, and then set it in her hand. "I'm going to run across the way and pick up a few things. Is there anything in particular you'd like?"

She thought for a minute, and I expected her to reiterate that she wasn't hungry. "A chai latte, please. Tell Rashid it's for me. He knows how I like it."

"How do you like it?" I asked, curious as to what options there were.

"Spicy and half-sweet." She rested her head against the sofa's cushion and closed her eyes again.

I couldn't keep myself from running my finger from her temple down her cheek. "Go ahead and sleep," I said when she opened her eyes and they met mine.

"I'll only be a few minutes, but ring me if you don't feel well."

"Okay," she whispered and turned away from me. I stood, knowing that if I didn't get out of here, I was going to lift Emerson into my arms and hold her as she slept. Never before had I felt such an overpowering need to take care of someone, and I found it rather disconcerting.

Once downstairs, I sent a text to Stephen, asking if it was normal for her to be so sleepy, and then dashed over to the market.

The man behind the counter ignored me until I asked for the chai. "It's for Emerson. She likes it spicy—"

"I know how she likes it," the man with a heavy Middle Eastern accent said as he walked out from behind the counter and toward the rear of the store.

"It needs to be decaffeinated," I added.

"Yes," he responded without turning around.

A few minutes later, he walked up with a lidded ceramic cup and looked at everything I had on the counter. "You take Emme her chai. I'll ring you up, and you pay when Rashid delivers."

"Are you Rashid?"

The man shook his head and looked at me as if I was daft. "Rashid is my son."

A few minutes after I returned, I realized that I hadn't given the man at the market Saint's apartment number. I was just about to leave to do so when Emerson's mobile rang.

"Hi," she answered. "Yes, I'm at Tommy's." There were a few seconds of silence on her end, but whatever the caller said, made her smile and her cheeks turn pink.

She ended the call and sat up. As soon as she did, she put her face in her hands. I bounded across the room to her. "What's wrong?"

She moved her hands and peered up at me. "I was hoping that when I opened my eyes, my mishap of this morning would've been a weird dream." She ran her hands over her hair. "I must look terrible."

On the contrary, she looked very much like she had the last time I saw her, and that was beautiful. I'd woken her with my mouth, watching her face as she came awake. I closed my eyes, only momentarily, pushing the memory away before my body reacted in an embarrassing way. "You look lovely," I murmured.

Seconds later, there was a knock at the door. When I opened it, I had an inkling of why she was concerned about her appearance.

Not that I usually took notice of other men, but it was impossible to ignore his attractiveness. He was like a walking sculpture—his facial features and body looked as though they'd been chiseled from stone. His hair was long on top and fell forward, and when he brushed it away and looked at me, I could see gold flecks in his hazel eyes. I felt Emerson's presence behind me.

"Emme," the man said, pushing past me. "What happened?"

I watched her cheeks flame and her eyes drop to the floor in a way that made me want to bend her to my will.

"I hit my head," she said.

"Oh no," *Rashid* responded, putting his arms around her. I hated the way she rested her cheek on his chest and closed her eyes. I might as well have been invisible as far as the two people standing a few feet from me were concerned. When I saw him bring his hand to her hair and stroke it, I was ready to rip his arm off.

"Your father said you'd have a bill," I snapped.

"Yes." He reached into his pocket but left one arm around Emerson.

"Did you bring the groceries?"

"They're in the hall," he responded before leaning forward and kissing *my* Emerson's forehead.

When he released her and walked toward me, I wanted to rush around him and reclaim her as my own. Instead, I pulled my billfold from my trouser pocket and handed him twenty dollars more than the tab came to. "I'll bring them in," I said as I followed him to the door, standing on the threshold so he couldn't step back inside. "Thank you," I managed to grunt at him before closing the door in his face.

6

Emerson

"The groceries," I reminded Lynx when he stepped away from the door he'd just slammed in my friend's face. What had that been about anyway?

"Right," he mumbled, pulling the door open. When he stepped inside with his arms full, I walked over to close the door behind him.

He unloaded the bags without looking up at me.

"Is everything okay?" I asked.

He raised his eyes. "Is Niven aware you have other boyfriends?"

If he didn't already have a scowl on his face, I would've laughed out loud. In fact, I should have. At the same time, I was confused. Why did he think Tommy was my boyfriend? I couldn't recall saying anything to give him that impression.

"Rashid is not my boyfriend per se. Neither is Tommy for that matter."

Lynx set the box of crackers he was holding on the counter. Slammed would be a better word; they had to be broken into thousands of pieces.

"What is he exactly, *per se*?"

This time, I did laugh. "Which one?"

"Rashid."

"He's just a friend."

"I doubt he feels that way," he muttered.

"*His* boyfriend would disagree."

"Oh." Lynx continued putting the groceries away. It was almost as if he was jealous, which was ludicrous, given I didn't register on his radar enough for him to even remember he'd spent a night with me.

"And Niven, does he realize the lackadaisical way you view your relationship with him?"

"We're friends," I mumbled, not understanding why Lynx was making this out to be more than it was.

Tommy and I had gone out for dinner several times, including more than once with Rashid and his long-term boyfriend. It was one of the things I liked best about my neighbor. Tommy seemed to be prejudice-free. Neither Rashid's ethnic background nor his sexual orientation bothered him.

I walked over to the sofa and picked up my cell phone, silently praying there would be some kind of response from my parents. When I saw there was a text message, I didn't feel as happy as I thought I would. If they were responding, that meant my time with Lynx would be coming to an end. I tapped the screen and couldn't contain my grin when I read the message from my mother.

Did you forget we're down the Cape this month?

I had forgotten. It was usually them looking for me, trying to coax me out of work. I was embarrassed to admit that I didn't pay much attention to their schedule, especially considering how much they'd sacrificed for me.

Do you want Dad to come into the city?

No, but thanks. I'll figure something else out. Enjoy your time at the beach.

Let me know if you change your mind.

I adored my parents. The three of us had always been close, especially after we lost my brother.

"Everything okay?" Lynx asked right before he took a bite out of an apple. I'd told him I wasn't hungry, but it looked so good. I couldn't take my eyes off his full lips as he slowly chewed. Maybe it wasn't the apple that looked good enough to eat as much as it was him.

He'd removed the long-sleeve dress shirt he wore to our meeting. Underneath, he had on a white v-neck that hugged his body, but not so tight that it looked like he was trying to show off his muscles. Although he had every right to. When he brought the apple to his mouth, flexing his biceps, I wanted to stalk across the floor and run my hands over them. I even licked my lips.

Once again catching me staring, he slowly lowered his arm. *Damn showoff.* "Are you certain you aren't hungry?"

Not just hungry, I was starving, but it had nothing to do with food. "That apple looks good. Did you get two?"

He smiled and returned to the kitchen, giving me another opportunity to ogle his ass. I doubted I'd ever seen a man who looked as good in trousers as he did. Except for maybe Rashid, but I'd never looked at him in the same way I was looking at Lynx.

I'd slipped earlier and called him that out loud, although it didn't appear he'd noticed. I had to keep reminding myself that as far as he knew, I wasn't aware that was another name he went by. Hoping it would prevent another slip, I began repeating *Lennox* in my head.

"Here." When he handed me the apple, his fingers brushed mine. Was it just me that felt a rush of longing whenever he touched me? Was the chemistry I felt between us really one-sided? Had he not noticed how flushed my face became when he spoke to me? Or how

I squeezed my thighs together when his skin touched mine? Was I really that forgettable? *Forgettable.*

"*Oh!* I forgot to mention that I heard from my parents." Was it also my imagination, or did the smile just leave his face? "They're at their house down the Cape this week. I'd forgotten that too."

"I see." I couldn't see his face when he turned around, but I could swear he was smiling again.

"I don't want you to think you're still on the hook for babysitting."

He rested his hands on the counter, and through his shirt, I could see his muscles tense. I stepped to the side so I could see his face, at least one side of it. His eyes were closed, and the muscles of his jaw were as tight as those of his back.

"Really, *Lennox.* I can just take a cab to my office, get my bags, and then have the same cab bring me back here. You *don't* have to hang out with me."

"No," he snapped.

Before I could argue, his cell phone rang and he walked into the bedroom.

God, why had I been so stupid to leave my keys in my bag? *Wait.* If I didn't know it would hurt really bad, I would've slammed my hand into my forehead. What was wrong with me? The super could get me into my apartment—it wasn't like it would be the first time.

I eased myself out of Tommy's door and called downstairs.

"Miss Emme, to what do I owe this pleasure?"

"Hi, Mr. Bridges. You aren't going to believe this, but I left my keys at the office."

He never seemed to mind my calling. It may have been because of the envelope of tip money I gave him every holiday. And in every holiday, I included things like National Pizza Day. That's how often Mr. Bridges had not only let me into my apartment, but offered to give me yet another set of spare keys.

I didn't actually lose them; I left them…not always in the same place, and not always in a place I could remember. When I found them—and I always did—I'd give that set to Mr. Bridges, so he'd have them the next time.

Fortunately, MIT's security only required my handprint, along with facial recognition. If I'd been responsible for keys to my building, or even my office, I probably would've lost my security clearance in the first month.

"Don't you worry. I'll be right up," said Mr. Bridges without a single grain of impatience evident in his voice.

"I'm sorry about this," I said when he met me at my door.

"You don't need to apologize to me, Miss Emme. It's always a pleasure to see you."

He held the door open for me, and I walked into the apartment, turning on the lamp in my living room.

There was something about overhead lighting I'd never cared for. This apartment had it, just like Tommy's did, but I never used it. I much preferred floor and table lamps.

The layout of our apartments was identical, but they couldn't have looked more different. His was modern and sleek. He'd left the concrete floors mostly bare while I'd covered every inch I could with thick, plush throw rugs. His furniture was all grays and tans with metal and glass tables and chairs. Mine was covered in prints and bright colors, and my tables and chairs were antique-looking wood.

The other difference I noticed, being in Tommy's apartment today, was that there wasn't a single thing out of place. Maybe because he was out of town, but something told me it wouldn't matter. Even if he'd been there this morning, I bet it would still have been spotless.

I liked having the things I loved out where I could see them. And since I *sometimes* ran late, it wasn't important to me that every single coffee cup end up in the dishwasher. Most mornings, I just rinsed out the one I'd used the day before—something that would make my mother absolutely insane. But my mother didn't live here. I did.

My guess was, like with most things, I took after my dad when it came to my ability to live happily amongst clutter. He probably didn't have any choice but to be neat and tidy, since unlike me, he did live with her.

"What happened?" Mr. Bridges asked, perhaps noticing the bandage that covered the staples in my head.

"A little mishap." That was becoming my new favorite word. *Mishap.* It said everything without needing further explanation. "Thank you again," I said when I saw the paperwork he was filling out on my kitchen counter.

"I've been meaning to tell you it isn't necessary for you to tip me, Miss Emme. It's my job to take care of the tenants of this building."

"I know that, but I like to do it. I know some of my neighbors make you cookies. I can assure you, you'd much rather have a modest tip than a batch of anything I'd make."

My mother was a fabulous cook, something that didn't get passed down to me. The last five times I'd tried to make something, I forgot that I had a pot on the stove or something in the oven. Poor Mr. Bridges had been forced to come up when my smoke detectors refused to stop blaring.

7

Lynx

"How's the patient?" Stephen asked when I answered his call.

"My worry is the amount of sleeping. Hence, the message."

"It isn't of concern as long as she doesn't have any of the other symptoms I mentioned."

"None so far." I checked the time; it was just after four. "Is your conference over, or are you on another break?"

"Over. I'm heading to Providence as soon as we ring off."

"Please give Nora my regards."

"I've an idea. Why don't you come down for dinner?"

"I've the patient to care for."

"Bring her."

"If she's feeling up to it."

"Brilliant. Nora will be so pleased to see you again. You will not believe how big the twins have gotten, and Brian is almost as tall as his mother."

The last I saw my cousin and his family was at Stephen and Nora's wedding. They'd waited to marry until after their twin girls were old enough to travel. Admittedly, I'd never dreamed Stephen would marry, let alone become a father, but I remembered marveling at the changes I witnessed in him. Only those who knew him well had any idea that he and Nora's son, Brian, weren't biologically related. The two were closer than any father and son I'd ever known.

"Sounds wonderful. Should I make a reservation somewhere?"

"No, no. Nora will insist on having you to the house. You know how she is."

Actually, I didn't. "I don't want to impose."

"You won't be. Truth be told, with the girls, a casual dinner at home is much easier for us to navigate."

"Thank you for the invitation, as long as you're sure we won't be putting Nora out."

"On the contrary. So, who is this woman whose head injury I treated?"

"Dr. Emerson Charles. She's with the International Policy Program."

"I'm intrigued."

As was I.

"What's her specialty?" Stephen asked.

"China."

"Right up your alley."

"On that subject, she isn't yet aware of my affiliation with MI6."

"Understood. We'll see you around six, then?"

When I came out of the bedroom, Emerson was nowhere to be found. I looked down the hall; the lavatory door was open, so she wasn't in there. I went in that direction anyway to check the back bedroom, which I knew was an office Saint kept locked. I tried turning the handle; it was locked as tight as it had been earlier.

If she wasn't in either of the bedrooms or the bathroom, she would've had to be in the main part of the house, and she wasn't. A sick feeling settled in the pit of my stomach.

Shoving my mobile into my pocket, I stalked out the door of the apartment in search of her. As I did, I saw an older gentleman coming out of her front door.

"Who are you?" I demanded, confronting him as he waited for the lift, immediately regretting the accusatory sound of my voice. "My apologies. Is Emerson in her apartment?"

"To answer your first question, I'm the super of the building," he said with an indulgent smile. "As such, I am sure you understand that I am not at liberty to say whether I let Miss Emme into her apartment or not."

When he winked, I smiled.

"Lennox Edgemon," I said, holding out my hand.

"Baxter Bridges, it's a pleasure to meet you. Friend of Saint's?"

His use of Niven's code name gave me pause. "That's right."

The lift dinged and he stepped inside, leaving me feeling as though Baxter Bridges knew a hell of a lot more about everything that happened in this building than he'd ever let on.

I stalked the rest of the way to Emerson's apartment, annoyed that she'd left without telling me. I knocked on the door—pounded, really—prepared to bust it down if she didn't answer before my count to five.

Moments later, the door flew open. "Lynx…uh, sorry…I mean Lennox. I, um, didn't want to interrupt while you were on the phone, but it dawned on me that the super could let me into my apartment."

Without invitation, I swept past her and into a living space that was set up identically to Saint's, but looked entirely different. Whereas the other apartment was sparsely furnished, sterile almost, Emerson's was cluttered, which I usually abhorred as much as small talk. But in this case, the space felt homey and warm. A place you could sink into and get lost in. Just like her.

"I would've come over to tell you," she murmured. "It's only been a few minutes."

"I was worried," I admitted, although I couldn't confess to the extent.

"I'm fine." She turned away from me like she had so many times before.

"Stephen called."

"Oh. Did you tell him I'm okay?" she asked over her shoulder before taking a seat on her sofa.

"He invited us to have dinner with him and his wife, Nora."

"Please give him my thanks, but I'll stay put."

"Very well." I pulled my mobile from my pocket to call and give my regrets.

"You should go and enjoy yourself, though."

"No," I said, shaking my head and tapping the screen to reach recent calls.

"But, I'm…fine."

"Fine," I said at the same time she did.

"Lennox," she said, standing and walking over to me. "This isn't necessary. I won't repeat how I feel since I've said it too many times already, but I'm an adult who is perfectly capable of taking care of myself."

I stared into her eyes, wanting nothing more than to pull her into my arms and kiss her. Before I thought better of it, I did. Pull her into my arms, that is. I stopped short of kissing her, but just barely.

At first, her body was stiff, but within seconds, she relaxed into me. I'd only been with her a few hours, and my resolve to make her think I didn't remember our night together was already weakening.

Unless I admitted that I'd never forgotten her, I couldn't kiss her. And I had to kiss her. I cupped her cheek with my palm and stared into her ocean eyes.

"I thought I'd never see you again."

Her eyes scrunched with confusion. "It was only a few minutes…"

I shook my head and pressed my lips to her ear, loving the shudder that shot through her body. She was just as responsive to me today as she had been three years ago, and my cock loved it. "It's been far longer than that, Emerson." I brought my lips to hers and parted them with my tongue. I couldn't wait patiently until she opened to me; I had to possess her immediately. I brought my other hand to her face and held her there, reminding myself not to push too hard when what I really wanted to do was devour her.

"Wait," Emerson said, pulling back. "You remember me?"

"How could I forget you?" I saw the question in her eyes, and as much as I wished she didn't have to ask, I knew she did, or I could be a man and tell her. "I recognized you this morning…in the lobby."

"But…why did you act like you didn't?"

"Because of what you do, and what I do too."

She took a step back and folded her arms. "I don't know what you do. In fact, until today, I didn't even know your last name."

"Nor I, yours." I took the same step forward that she'd taken back and unfolded her arms, putting one hand and then her other on my shoulders. "I woke up and you were gone." I leaned forward and kissed the tip of her nose. "My disappointment was profound."

"Do you really expect me to believe that?"

Other than keeping up the charade that I didn't remember her, there was nothing I'd done that warranted her distrust. "Why would you doubt it?"

"Because you're…"

I smiled and captured her mouth a second time. Maybe I shouldn't have kissed her again, but I was powerless not to.

I'd kissed other women in the last three years, but never anyone like her. I remembered more than her scent. The look on her face when our bodies first came together, the wonder of her, stretched out naked before me…I remembered it all, especially how her lips felt when they touched mine. For three years, I'd looked for another kiss that felt like hers, and until today, I thought I'd never find one.

"Wait," she said, pushing away from me.

I knew exactly what she was about to say, and wished I could stop her. Instead, I said it for her. "Niven."

"Niven? Oh, you mean Tommy."

Right. *Tommy.* They even had pet names for each other. As difficult as it was, I released her. More difficult, though, was stopping myself from asking about their relationship.

"That wasn't what I was going to say." She tapped her mouth with her fingertip.

"What were you going to say?"

She cocked her head and backed up. "Now I can't remember."

I reached out for one more touch, but she was too far away. "I'm not sorry."

She spun on her heel. "What did you say?"

I looked away, ashamed, but at the same time, I would kiss her again—more—if she'd let me. "I don't regret kissing you, Emerson. But if you and Niven are in a relationship. I'll respect that."

"Relationship?"

"Seeing each other. Whatever you want to call it."

"I don't understand."

I studied her. Was I wrong somehow?

I felt as confused as she seemed to be. However, if she felt no particular loyalty to a man I knew would make the most of any opportunity another woman presented to him, then why was I worried about it?

"Go with me tonight. Please," I said, holding out my hand. She didn't take it, but she nodded.

8

Emerson

"You look fantastic," Lynx said when I answered the door to my apartment thirty minutes later.

When he'd offered to leave me on my own to shower and change, I had a flashback to our one night together, and how at midnight, we'd shared a candlelit bath in his room's claw-foot tub.

"Shall we?" Lynx asked, jarring me out of my memory…fantasy…memorable fantasy.

Stepping into the elevator, thoughts of our bath were immediately replaced by memories of a very different elevator ride than the one we were taking now.

Once the doors closed behind Lynx and me that night, he'd pushed me up against the wall, parted my legs with his knee, and ground his thigh against my wetness.

"I'm going to fuck you senseless," he'd said, and I'd almost orgasmed from that alone.

I took a deep breath and let my eyes wander the length of him. He'd changed into a black t-shirt similar to the white one he had on earlier, and instead of dress pants, he wore jeans. He looked so fucking hot I could barely stop myself from pushing him up against this elevator wall.

The door opened, and the harsh light of day shook me out of my lustful stupor. Lynx motioned for me to go ahead of him, and every so often, I could feel his fingers brush against the curve of my spine. He'd done the same thing that night. I shuddered.

"Everything okay?" he asked.

"It's fine," I said, raising my eyes to catch the lip twitch and smirk he quickly tried to mask.

A car similar to the one that had taken us to MIT this morning and then driven us back later, sat at the curb in front of the building. Thankfully, though, Speed Racer was nowhere to be found.

He held my door open, leaning in close enough that he could've kissed the side of my neck, but he didn't. My disappointment was palpable.

We'd been on the road for at least fifteen minutes, and neither of us spoke. The longer the silence dragged on, the more I thought about why he'd acted like he didn't recognize me. Part of me felt angry, but did I have any right to be?

Had I said, "Hey, Lynx, you were the best fuck of my life. Why don't you remember me?" Nope. Did I remind him we met in the bar of my hotel and within an hour of meeting we were tearing one another's clothes off? Nope. I hadn't done that either.

He'd said his reason for not acknowledging he knew me was because of what I did. And what he did. What did that mean? And why hadn't I asked? So I did.

He took a deep breath and looked everywhere but at me. I sensed this was bigger than, "What do you do for a living?"

"The position I'm in…scratch that." He took another deep breath. "I know what really goes on at IPP. All of it, Emerson. However, until this morning, I had no idea you," his gaze traveled the length of me, and I shivered, "were Dr. Charles."

"And now that you do?"

"You should be aware that I'm in Boston undercover on behalf of MI6."

Something else occurred to me. "Tommy is MI6 too, isn't he?"

Lynx nodded. "Although in our world, he's known as Saint."

"And you're known as Lynx?"

"That's right."

"Were you with MI6 three years ago?"

"Yes."

"Did you try to find me? The next day?"

He shook his head and looked away.

He hadn't, but I already knew that. The only reason my insecure self could conjure was that it hadn't mattered enough for him to bother.

"You're wrong."

I'd been looking out the side window but turned to face him. "What did you say?"

"What you're thinking is wrong."

"How do you know what I'm thinking?"

Lynx reached over and brushed the bare skin of my thigh with the back of his hand. "Because I do."

"Why didn't you try?"

"Because I woke and you were gone. Because you were a wide-eyed twenty-five-year-old on your first time in London, at a conference you didn't believe you belonged attending."

"You remember all that?"

"I remember everything, Emerson." He slid his hand down so it rested above my knee. "Why did you leave?"

Why had I? To avoid embarrassment. To avoid the ugly morning after when the hotter-than-hell guy wishes the girl had just left rather than having to endure an awkward conversation in which he'd say he'd call, yet never would.

"Here we are," he said, pulling into the driveway before I had a chance to answer. The suddenness of our arrival jarred me.

Why had I agreed to this? How would he introduce me? Would I be the crazy woman who spilled water on him and then bonked her head on the table, requiring Stephen to give her medical care when he was really in Boston to attend a conference?

Lynx unfastened his seatbelt but didn't get out of the car. Instead, he took my hand in his. "They're going to love you."

"I feel so…"

"What?"

I shook my head.

"I'll tell you how I feel. I'm happy you agreed to come with me."

"Who will you tell them I am?"

"A woman that I've recently reconnected with. One I'm very anxious to get to know better."

"Lynx?" I said, looking down at our hands. "When do you think Tommy—Saint—will be back?"

The look on his face made me wish I hadn't asked.

"I don't know."

—:—

Dinner with Stephen and his wife was delightful. While initially I felt like an imposition, Nora put me to work almost immediately, perhaps sensing I'd be more comfortable if I was doing rather than watching.

"I have to warn you, I'm a bit of a klutz." I pointed to my head.

She washed her hands, dried them, and refilled my wine glass. "The first time I met Stephen's parents, I dropped an entire carton of eggs on his mother's feet."

I choked on my wine when I laughed, which was better than spitting it out, which was what I almost did. "You're kidding."

"They surprised us, Stephen really. I don't think they expected he'd invite them to dinner here. Let me tell you, it was disastrous. On top of everything else, Stephen had planned to propose to me that night, and I was pregnant with the twins."

"Wow." I had nothing else. I couldn't even imagine what that night must've been like.

"It all worked out in the end," she said, looking into the other room where her husband sat on the floor, chatting and laughing with Lynx while he and Brian played with the two girls.

"Your children are lovely."

Her cheeks pinkened, and she smiled. "Thank you. Eleanor is so much like Stephen. Elizabeth is more like me, and Brian has absolutely taken to being a big brother. I pity any boy who tries to date either of the girls once they're old enough. Between their father and their brother, their dates will not stand a chance." She smiled again and shook her head. "I'd best stop talking. This chicken isn't going to cook itself."

Part of me wished we'd ordered in, just so she would keep talking. I didn't recall meeting another woman who put me so at ease.

"Let's eat," Nora shouted out to Stephen and Lynx as she directed me to the other side of the house where the dining room was located.

"Something smells appetizing," Lynx whispered, coming up behind me, resting both hands on my waist, and practically burying his nose in my hair. "I know what I'd like for dessert."

If he didn't have his hands on my waist, I might've slid straight to the floor when my knees went weak. My eyes rolled back in my head as the memory of waking up with his head between my legs sent an electrical current ricocheting straight to my clit.

"Quit that," murmured Stephen, bumping Lynx as he walked past us. "If you give Nora any ideas, before you know it, you'll be babysitting the twins after dining alone."

Nora came around the opposite side of me. "The men in their family claim God-like irresistibility," she murmured.

"Try to tell me that isn't the case," said Stephen, kissing her neck.

I wiggled out of Lynx's grasp when I saw Brian walk around us and take a seat at the table, seemingly ignoring the adults behaving like adolescents.

By the time we left, I felt as though I'd known both Stephen and Nora for years rather than just a couple of hours.

She and I agreed to meet for lunch in Boston one day the following week when Stephen was off-duty and before Brian's school vacation ended.

"I knew you and Nora would hit it off," Lynx said on the drive back.

"She's great, and so is Stephen."

"He and I haven't spent much time together since we were kids, but when we're together again, it's like no time has passed at all." He smiled at me. "Kind of like it is with you."

Was it? The only thing between us had been sex. Mind-blowing, life-altering—for me anyway—hot-as-fuck sex. That had been it. There hadn't been time for anything else.

"What's troubling you? Headache?"

"No. I'm...*fine*."

He laughed.

Before we left, Stephen asked several questions about how I was feeling, checked my *laceration*, and told me he doubted I had a concussion. However, he did remind me what to be aware of in the event I began having symptoms. I'd thought we were alone until I looked over and saw Lynx standing in the doorway.

When our eyes met, I'd wondered what he was thinking. Stephen admitted he doubted I had a concussion, so there was no reason for him to babysit me for the next few hours. What would we do when he took me home? Would we say goodnight and go our separate ways?

"If it's not a headache, tell me what is bothering you."

It took me a long time to answer as I sorted through what I was feeling. Lynx reached over and brushed the side of my leg like he had earlier, but didn't say a word.

"I got carried away," I finally said.

"By?"

"Stephen and Nora were so welcoming, but I'm not sure meeting her next week is a good idea."

"Hmm." It was dark in the car, but I could see his eyes scrunch and his forehead furrow. "She'll be disappointed."

I doubted that. Someone like Nora would have countless friends. I was different. Work had become my bestie.

I thought about Tommy again. He was my friend and I missed him. He was out of town so often, that when he was home, I didn't feel guilty about leaving the office earlier than I normally would when he invited me to join him for dinner.

I hadn't even begun to process that he worked for MI6. Why hadn't he let on? He knew what I did for a living—at least in theory. But had he really kept it a secret? Hadn't he given me enough clues that if I had been paying attention, I should've picked up on it?

There was something about the way Lynx said he didn't know when Tommy would return that gave me the impression he was worried. I wouldn't ask him about it again now, though. The mood had already shifted enough because of my melancholia.

"Why don't you see how it goes?"

"What do you mean?"

"I truly believe Nora is looking forward to spending an afternoon with you. My prediction is you'll both enjoy yourselves."

I didn't know what to say in response, but nothing needed to be decided tonight.

Lynx moved his hand so it rested right above my knee, also like he'd done earlier. "I enjoyed our evening very much."

"I did too," I admitted. I didn't remember laughing as much as I did tonight since before my brother died.

Lynx and Stephen had been playful, neither shy about making nearly everything a sexual innuendo, although not until Brian had left the table, I'd noticed.

It reminded me of how Lynx had been that night at the bar. Playful, teasing, flirtatious, and finally seductive—he'd been so self-assured that I would've put my hand in his and followed him anywhere.

I closed my eyes—remembering. Maybe he'd been right not to try to find me. One perfect night. That's what we'd had. Instead of wondering what might have been, I should simply be thankful it had happened at all.

9

Lynx

The way Emerson shifted in her seat and looked down at my hand on her knee, it was easy to assume she was thinking about the same thing I was—the night that I'd never been able to forget.

Was it because she'd left before dawn? Had she stayed, would I have felt differently? As it was, the memory of Emerson took on a life of its own. She became the one who'd gotten away.

I'd lied to her earlier when she asked why I hadn't tried to find her. I had. In fact, I knew she'd left before the end of the conference, and why.

I often wondered if I ever saw her again, if she'd live up to my memory of her. She did. In fact, she was so much more. She was beautiful, like Irish had said. She was also charming and witty, extraordinarily intelligent, and had fit in with Stephen and Nora like I'd hoped she would.

While this morning I thought she was too thin, her tits maybe too small, when she came out in the dress she was wearing, my eyes nearly popped out of my head, and my cock almost pushed through the zipper of my jeans.

The sleeveless dress hugged her slight frame, and while it didn't dip far enough to show much cleavage, the swell of her breasts made me want to lean over and lick them. That it fell midway down her legs, had me imagining what she might be wearing under it. Lace knickers? A thong perhaps? Or maybe nothing at all.

I groaned, removing my hand from her leg. If I hadn't, I would've gone farther, letting my fingers explore the heat between her thighs. It was all I could do to stop myself from imagining what I'd find. Would she be wet? I knew she would be. When I slipped my finger under the drenched material, would she spread her legs for me? When I reached her pussy, would it be bare like it had been three years ago?

Remembering her reaction to Rashid and how she'd demurely looked at the floor when he'd questioned her, I wondered how she'd react if I told her to—demanded that she—raise her dress and spread her legs? What if, at the same time, I pulled the bodice down so both her tits and pussy were on view for me?

I tried to focus on the road, and even though I could feel Emerson's eyes on me, I didn't allow myself another look.

"Lynx?"

"I can't look at you at the moment, my darling. My ability to drive depends on my keeping my eyes off of you."

"You missed the exit."

How did she make those four words sound like the sexiest I'd ever heard? "Fuck," I swore under my breath, and then had to look at her to see if she'd heard me.

Her eyes were hooded. Had she been able to read my thoughts? Did she want my hands on her as much as I wanted to run them over every inch of her bare skin? Thrust my fingers into her pussy while I demanded she pinch her nipples for me? I groaned and adjusted my trousers as she watched.

"Do you have any idea how much I want to fuck you right now, Emerson? How much I want to spread your legs and taste the sweetness between them?"

She shuddered like she had so many times in the last few hours. It was all I could do not to pull the car over and rip her dress from her body.

Somehow, although I doubt I could duplicate our drive, I got us to her building. I pulled up to the front and was about to get out to open her door, when I saw a man standing near the entrance.

"What is Paxon doing here?" she murmured, obviously noticing him at the same time I did.

I didn't know, but by the look on his face, I could tell his reason wasn't a good one.

He walked over and opened Emerson's door, glaring at me as he held out his hand to help her out. After he had, Irish stuck his head inside. "Where have you been?"

I didn't care for his tone even a little. "Dinner, not that it's any of your business."

"We need to talk," he seethed.

I looked beyond him to where Emerson waited just inside the glass doors of her building.

"She knows who I am," I told him.

"*About Saint,*" he spat, slamming the passenger door before he stalked away.

"What's going on?" Emerson asked when I joined her in the lobby.

"I believe Mr. Warrick has news of Saint."

Other than looking into my eyes, she had little reaction. As we rode the lift to her floor, I noticed her chewing the inside of her lip.

"Is Tommy in danger?"

"I fear he is."

"Paxon isn't an assistant analyst, is he?"

"He's not."

"Does he also work for MI6?"

"No. CIA."

Emerson nodded and continued chewing the inside of her lip, processing what I'd just told her.

"Does the danger Tommy is in have anything to do with China?"

"Yes," I admitted.

"My work with Dr. Benjamin specifically?"

"Yes," I answered for the second time. As much as I wanted to reassure her, I had to meet with Irish first and find out what was so urgent that he'd been waiting outside Emerson's building.

"Goodnight," she said when we exited the lift and I walked toward Saint's apartment rather than hers. "Thank you for a lovely evening." She opened her door and then closed it behind her without taking another look at me.

I stalked over to Saint's apartment, ready to tear into Irish, but stopped abruptly. As I'd told Emerson, he was not MI6. He worked for the CIA. If there was anyone I should be tearing into, it was his boss.

Sumner Copeland was a man I knew well. We'd risen through the ranks of our respective agencies at the same time and had always been able to work out our differences even when our employers couldn't.

"Lynx, I've been expecting this call."

"How are you, Cope?"

"Working too much. Don't see my family nearly enough. You know how that is."

I did understand the part about working too much, but outside of my brother, who worked as much or more than I did, I didn't have anyone in my life who would miss me if I weren't around.

"You said you've been expecting my call. Why?" I asked.

"What has Irish told you?"

"Nothing yet."

"We've received a brush pass from Saint."

"And?" Jesus, why hadn't Irish said so straight away?

"He's tracked Benjamin into Hong Kong."

That didn't come as a surprise. The man had been hell-bent on using the Hong Kong protests as a stage to further his agenda by way of calling attention to China's human rights exploitation.

"There's more."

"Go on."

"I'm quoting here, Lynx, so please understand that the phraseology comes from Saint himself."

"Very well."

"The message reads, 'We don't protect them because they are weak. We protect them because they are strong, and strong people make enemies.'"

It wasn't unlike Saint to use obscure quotes as messages. He liked to dangle clues without enough bloody information for anyone to decipher it—a trait I was beginning to abhor.

"Any idea what he's referring to?" Cope asked.

"Not straight away."

"Irish thinks it's a reference to Dr. Charles."

There was a certain amount of logic behind that line of thinking. While not as publicly outspoken as Dr. Benjamin, Emerson was among the leading critics of the Chinese. The policy she wrote often suggested trade sanctions designed to bring them to their knees economically.

Cope went on. "I'm going to tell you something that needs to stay confidential between us. Can you give me your word?"

"You have it."

"Tread carefully, Lynx."

"For bloody sake, Cope, get to the point."

"Irish believes you pose a threat to Dr. Charles."

"Pull him," I spat.

"I won't do that."

"Then I'll go over your head."

"He's a good man, Lynx. Misguided at times, but nonetheless, a good man and an outstanding agent. I believe his heart lies in protecting Dr. Charles."

"I'll not have someone working against me on my own mission, Cope."

"Then convince him that you both have the same agenda—protecting Dr. Charles."

I shouldn't have to convince anyone of a bloody thing.

"Irish may have developed feelings for the doctor."

Yes, he'd mentioned that himself, but it didn't make the situation any better.

"Work with him, Lynx. Use it to your advantage."

I didn't have much of a choice, did I? Other than going above Cope's head, but did I truly have cause?

"By the way," he said. "I had a conversation earlier with Z. He'll be expecting your call as well."

I was a card-carrying spy, and even I was annoyed by this subterfuge.

I rang off my call with Cope and immediately placed one to my boss, Z Alexander, Chief of the U.K.'s Secret Intelligence Service, aka MI6.

"Lynx, I was about to ring you," he said.

"Second time I've heard that this evening. I've just finished speaking with Cope."

"You're aware of Saint's brush pass, then?"

"Affirmative."

"The bloody wanker and his quotes. Why didn't he say what needed to be said straight out?" Saint had been walking on thin ice with Z before this mission. The only thing standing between him and unemployment was my personal assurance I'd bring him around. I was beginning to wish I hadn't made that commitment.

"He and Benjamin are in Hong Kong. Shall I assemble a team to go in for them?"

"I've decided we should go off the books for this one."

"I don't necessarily disagree, but what's your reasoning?"

"Something is rotten in the state of Denmark."

I concurred with his Hamlet reference. Everything was not as it seemed.

"Are your concerns within MI6?"

"Not presently."

"Who are you thinking?"

"Your call, Lynx, but I do have a recommendation."

"Go on."

"You've worked with Decker Ashford in the past."

"Many times." The American was a bloody genius when it came to security technology—aka spyware.

"You know about the new group, then?"

I laughed, of course I did, and Z knew it. My younger brother, Keon, a former MI5 agent, was one of the four founding partners, along with a high-ranking MI6 agent and another MI5 agent.

The aforementioned Ashford had always refused to do more than freelance contracting work. I was anxious to ask what had made him change his mind about becoming a permanent part of this particular team.

In any event, while this was a big op for a new team, collectively they were hardly unseasoned recruits.

"I'll ring them."

"Glad you agree, Lynx," Z said as if I'd had a choice.

10

Emerson

I was stunned it hadn't occurred to me that Paxon wasn't who he pretended to be. I'd worked with the CIA a number of times. Why hadn't it dawned on me until now that that's what he was?

He'd shown up nine months ago, within a few days of Tommy moving into the building, not that I'd noticed at the time. There was something about that coincidence I was missing. What, though?

Lynx had confirmed that Tommy's disappearance had something to do with my work with Dr. Benjamin in regard to China. Again, what?

The Chinese had been my main focus since joining the IPP. I was offered the position because of my research into the risks associated with our dependence on their exports—particularly generic prescription drugs.

While some considered my viewpoints alarmist, given the growing trade war and animosity between our two countries, I believed the United States' utter dependence on China for basic medicines posed a significant national security threat. The subject of my doctoral dissertation was how China's drug manufacturing dominance gave it a "nuclear" option in the ongoing trade war. Millions of Americans could die without access to lifesaving medications if China decided to weaponize its drug-making.

Considering MIT was aggressive in hiring me away from Stanford, I initially felt vindicated in the face of my naysayers. Any sense of victory I felt was soon replaced by dread when I realized that my theories were only the tip of the iceberg when it came to the threat China posed not just to the United States, but to the world.

I'd been with IPP a little over a year when, six months ago, Dr. Benjamin contacted me directly, asking for a meeting. I'd had to clear it with the head of the program, but given the request had also come to him by way of England's prime minister, he was quick to approve it.

If I thought I'd stumbled on a significant Chinese threat, what I learned from Dr. Benjamin had made my blood run cold. So much so, that there were times I wanted to walk away from my job and find a teaching position in some small college town off the world's radar.

I couldn't, though. The reason I'd begun researching China's role in the U.S. pharmaceuticals in the first place was personal. At the time, my main concern related to their import of illicit fentanyl and the painkiller's analogues.

Fentanyl was one hundred times stronger than morphine. It was given to relieve severe pain, like after surgery. The addictive nature of the drug resulted in it being responsible for over fifty thousand deaths this year alone in the U.S. Three years ago, while I was at the conference in London, my older brother became one of those statistics.

He'd gotten hooked on it after he had knee surgery following a football injury. The autopsy my parents had asked be performed, indicated that the amount of the drug found in his body had depressed his respiratory system to the point of failure, leading to his fatal overdose.

I was wrecked by his death. More so because I'd been out of the country at the time. Shortly after leaving Lynx's bed and returning to my room, I received the call from my parents, informing me of what happened, and had made arrangements to fly home immediately.

Even if Lynx had tried to find me, I was already gone.

The days and weeks that followed were among the worst of my life. For me, losing a sibling had been devastating; for my parents, it had been their worst nightmare realized.

The truth was, my night with Lynx helped me through it. Whenever things became too much for me to handle and I had to check out for a few minutes, I let my mind wander to memories of the hot Englishman I met in a bar, followed by a wild night of sex. It was the craziest thing I'd ever done, and somehow, I thought if he'd known, my brother would have given me an enthusiastic pat on the back for doing something so far out of my comfort zone.

In the same way it helped my parents and me navigate his addiction, counseling got us through my brother's death. It hadn't been easy then, and it still wasn't. I felt his loss on a daily basis. Things happened that I'd want to share with him, or I'd see something that reminded me of him—there were countless ways he came to mind. Each time, it felt like a knife in my heart.

I heard a knock at the door and walked over to open it, expecting to see Lynx. Instead, it was Paxon.

"Can I come in?"

"Of course," I said, stepping aside and then looking beyond him.

"He's not with me. I asked for a few minutes on my own."

I nodded. "Can I get you anything?"

"No. I'm here to apologize."

"There's nothing to apologize for. You're doing your job."

Tonight was the first I'd seen him wear anything besides a long-sleeve dress shirt, and was stunned to see that both of his arms were covered with tattoos. His body, like Lynx's, was muscular, something I also hadn't noticed as much when he wore business attire.

"Sometimes, the hardest part of being undercover is getting to know the people you work with, and then feeling regret that the role you play in their lives isn't real."

"I understand," I murmured. "What happens now?"

"Nothing changes, except that you know who I really am, and that makes it harder on you. On the other hand, both Lynx and I are going to ask you to help us, and that we can be upfront about it, makes it easier for all three of us."

"Is anyone else in the office aware of who you really are?"

"Only Dr. Baker."

That made sense. As the head of the International Policy Program, it would've been necessary for Dr. Baker to approve the CIA and MI6 working undercover within our walls.

"Are you going to tell me what's happening with Tommy, or is Lynx?"

"He will."

I saw a glimpse of something on his face that he quickly masked. Perhaps whatever that was about, Lynx would explain to me also.

"Thank you for coming over to talk to me rather than waiting until tomorrow when it might be awkward."

"It's late. I should go."

I walked Paxon to the door, but before he could walk out, I put my hand on his shoulder. When he turned, I hugged him. I could feel the relief in his muscles when he returned my embrace.

"I'll talk to you later," he said, stepping away from me.

Interesting word choice. Not "see you tomorrow."

He and Lynx made eye contact when he brushed past Paxon, who stood waiting for the elevator, but neither spoke.

I closed the door behind us once he stepped inside.

"Can I get you anything?" I asked him like I'd asked Paxon.

"A glass of wine if you have it."

I held up two bottles, and Lynx pointed to the red. I handed him a glass and motioned to the sofa. When I sat beside him, he stretched his arm out behind me.

"It's after midnight. You've had a long day," he said, brushing his fingertips along my shoulder.

"I won't be able to sleep until you tell me what's going on. That's if you're permitted to."

When he sighed and scrubbed his face with his hand, I stood.

"Wait." He grasped my wrist, and I sat back down. "As you're aware, Saint's mission, as well as Irish's, is highly classified."

"Irish?"

"Right. Sorry. Paxon."

"Not an assistant analyst, an agent. Someone who has worked in my midst, with whom I shared my opinions and beliefs. Who in turn will likely use them against me." I hated being deceived, especially when so much of my work involved interacting with high-ranking government officials. Why hadn't the CIA, or even my own boss, trusted me not to divulge the identity of the undercover agent? It was something they'd have to do now.

He ran his finger down the side of my face. "You're feeling betrayed." Again, I found myself wondering how the man was seemingly able to read my thoughts.

"Tell me what you can about Tommy."

"He was here undercover, essentially on Dr. Benjamin's detail. But for other reasons too. I'm here because he's been out of contact for over two weeks."

"What's different tonight? If you're here because he's been out of contact and it's been two weeks, why was Paxon waiting when we got back?"

"He received word of a brush pass—in this case, agent to agent."

"Tommy handed something off to another agent?"

"That's right. Not MI6, CIA."

Which was logical. If the brush pass had happened between two MI6 agents, Lynx would've been contacted rather than Paxon.

"What was it?"

"Information that could lead us to his whereabouts."

I wasn't going to ask anything more, and I hoped he didn't tell me. While my role was as an analyst and strategist, I knew enough about the game to understand that knowing too much would put me in danger.

Something else dawned on me. "Is Dr. Benjamin missing as well?"

"Yes."

"What's the next step?"

"I've been tasked with putting a team together to find them."

"Will you be on that team?"

Lynx shook his head.

I hated asking my next question. "Are you returning to the U.K.?"

"Not yet."

"But you will soon?"

Lynx

I had no definitive answer to Emerson's question. I took another sip of wine and mulled over how much more I should tell her.

"Emerson?" I whispered when she rested her head on my shoulder.

"Hmm?"

"You're exhausted. You should get some sleep."

When she didn't make a move, neither did I. Having her beside me was temporary; I should take as much of it as she'd allow. I breathed her in, like I always did when she was near me. If only doing so didn't drive the want I felt for her sky-high.

I heard her take a deep breath and then let it out slowly. "It started out that Tommy and I would have dinner together when he was in town."

I closed my eyes, wishing I could stop her. The last thing I wanted to hear about was Saint. Earlier today, I'd been ready to rip a gay man's arms off for comforting her. Whatever she told me about my missing agent might compel me to let him remain so.

"As you know, the man is charm personified. I mean, he's like a movie star. Maybe he should be the next James Bond, it wouldn't exactly be a stretch. I mean, it's his real job, right? Plus, he already dresses the part. He could probably win an award for the best-dressed man in all of England."

I groaned inwardly. Was she truly this oblivious to what her words were doing to me? However, maybe hearing about how wonderful she believed Saint to be, would make it easier for me to stop myself from picking her up, carrying her into the bedroom, and driving every thought of Mister Charm Personified straight out of her head.

She looked up at me with wide eyes, as though she realized she was rambling. "Anyway, he and I are very different," she murmured. "I'm sure you know my…background."

"Yes." Emerson would be well aware that I knew Dr. Charles' *background*. She graduated from secondary school at the age of fifteen and was accepted into Stanford University, where she completed her studies, including graduate and post-graduate degrees. Eighteen months ago, she was hired by MIT as a research analyst and political strategist. However, I had no idea what that had to do with Saint.

"Other than you, the men I've dated haven't been like Tommy. I mean, you and I didn't date, but…" Her cheeks flushed. "When Tommy kissed me, I was stunned, to be honest. That someone like him would be interested in someone like me…I found it…surprising."

"Emerson…"

I couldn't bear to listen to another word. She cared about Saint, and he, her. I didn't like to think of myself as the kind of man who would poach another man's woman, nor would I put Emerson in such an unfair position when she was simply being honest with me.

"Yes?"

"This conversation is unnecessary. If you think you owe me an explanation for any relationship you're in now, or ever, you're mistaken." I stood and stalked out before she could utter anything more.

The moment I entered Saint's apartment, I had to get out. What had happened within these walls? Had he and Emerson talked, laughed together, kissed, touched? Had he fucked her here?

I stalked to the lift, punching the button over and over, finally deciding I couldn't wait and took the stairs instead.

"Watch where you're going!" someone shouted at me as I came out the side door of the building and into a throng of people. I stood out of the way until enough had passed that I could cross Boylston.

As I walked past the corner market, my gaze met Rashid's, further raising my ire.

How in the hell could I feel so possessive of a woman with whom I'd spent less time than either Saint or Rashid had?

"You look like I feel," I heard someone say, and looked up to see Irish raising a pint in my direction. That was exactly what I fancied now, perhaps with several shots of Irish whiskey to chase it.

After stopping by the bar, I took my pint and shot out to the patio where Irish sat.

"I didn't expect to see you again tonight," he said as I pulled out a chair and sat down.

"Nor I, you." What was he doing here, anyway?

"I guess I know why you asked how close Emme and I are this morning."

"It isn't what you think."

Irish shook his head. "I said I'd like that to change once the mission was over. You decided not to wait."

I was in no mood to justify anything between Emerson and myself, particularly since it appeared that Saint had bested both Irish and I for her attention.

"We've met once before," I told him, regretting that I did as soon as the words left my mouth. What happened between me and the woman I could see gazing out her window at us was none of Irish's business.

"Have you come to any decisions about who to use for Saint and Dr. Benjamin's extraction?" he asked, following my line of sight.

I nodded. "A private firm."

"Who's heading it up?"

"Decker Ashford and Cortez DeLéon."

"Rile?"

"Yes."

"Heard they started a new group. Some bullshit name like the Invincibles or something."

"That is correct," I said, deciding not to comment on his disparaging remark, in part because I agreed with it. Their official name was the Invincible Intelligence and Security Group.

"What's the plan?" he asked.

As luck would have it, when I rang Decker Ashford earlier, he informed me the rest of the team was with him in Texas. "They'll be here in the morning."

Irish took another drink of his beer. "About Emme—"

"She was seeing Saint."

Irish's mouth hung open. "No shit?"

I didn't respond.

"How much does she know?" he asked.

"Only that there was a brush pass, but not the details of it." I was in no position to give Irish orders; however, I hoped he wouldn't let on what she had no reason to know—at least not yet.

He drained the rest of the beer from his glass and set it on the table. "Early start tomorrow," he muttered by way of explanation I suppose. I nodded my head slowly, but my eyes stayed focused on the beautiful figure who appeared again in the window.

Once Irish was gone, I slowly raised my hand, just to see if she'd acknowledge I did so. Her only response was to walk away.

"Can I bring you anything else?" asked the scant-ily clad barmaid, who I hadn't noticed standing near the table.

"More of the same," I said, pointing to the two empty glasses.

"Are you a friend of Irish's?"

"No," I answered, hoping to ward off further small talk.

When I saw the lights in Emerson's apartment go off a few minutes later, I wished I hadn't ordered another round.

12

Emerson

After the door closed behind him, I sat stunned. Had Lynx let me finish, I would've told him that I didn't know why he thought Tommy and I were dating. He'd kissed me once. I'd freaked out on him. End of story.

I suppose I should be thankful he left before I could humiliate myself more than I already had today. Lynx had made it clear our one night would be a once-in-a-lifetime night. I could handle that, but why, on our drive back from Stephen and Nora's, did he ask if I knew how much he wanted to fuck me?

I got up and poured myself another glass of wine and walked over to the window. I looked down on the people walking on Boylston. There must've been an event at Fenway tonight based on the number of people walking past my building to the T.

Through the windows of the market across the street, I could see that both Rashid and his father were working tonight. Next door, the diner that catered to late-night crowds had a line of people waiting to get in, and at the bar next door to it, a man who looked a lot like Paxon was seated at one of the outdoor tables. I knew it was him when Lynx joined him.

Any other night, I'd go downstairs, walk across the street, and ask why they hadn't invited me to join them for a beer. Not tonight, though. Everything had changed in my little world. No one was who they said they were, not even me.

I sat down and thought about the last time I saw Tommy. We'd had dinner at a Brazilian place off of Park Drive. It had become one of my favorites after he'd taken me there the first time.

Closing my eyes, I rested my head against the sofa and let my mind replay one of the last conversations he and I had. His sapphire-blue eyes were piercing as he took in every word I said and processed it.

I could never get enough air into my lungs when I was with the man—I'd never spent time with someone as classically handsome. If Lynx reminded me of a young Pierce Brosnan, Tommy was more Chris Hemsworth with a Robert Downey Jr. smirk. He was the kind of man who made heads turn when he walked into a room, not just by his movie-star good looks, but also his aura.

As usual, he'd been dressed in a suit. I'd rarely seen him wear anything else, odd as it seemed in the heat of summer, on him it worked. When he took off his jacket, his shirt was perfectly pressed in the same way no strand was out of place of his slicked-back sandy-blond hair.

It was his voice, though, that made me raise my head the first time we met in the hallway of our building. It was soft with an aristocratic lilt.

"I'm Niven St. Thomas," he'd said that morning. "And you are?"

I'd told him my name was Emerson Charles, and from that day, he'd called me Charlie.

The one and only time Tommy had kissed me, I was shocked, but not so much so that I didn't notice what an expert kisser he was. While Lynx's were impassioned, Tommy's was technically perfect, measured, elegant, the kind the hero gave the heroine in the old movies I loved so much.

"Tell me about your work," he'd said the first night he invited me to dinner.

I found myself telling him about my brother's addiction and how it had led me to fight against drug smuggling—fentanyl primarily.

"It's war," he'd murmured. "Whether it's the kind we fight with armies to defend our land, or against gangs, or even countries that seek to do us harm by means not considered an act of war, that's what it remains." The solemnity of his words in contrast to his usually affable demeanor, stunned me.

"Tell me about your work, Tommy," I'd said.

"I fight whatever war needs to be fought," he'd responded, shifting his gaze away from me.

His words made so much more sense to me now, knowing that he was with MI6. He fought whatever battles his country asked him to, just like Lynx and Paxon.

There was something about being around Tommy that made me feel safe, and as unsettled as I was, I wished so much that I could talk to him, see him standing outside my door, feel his arms around me as he told me everything was going to be okay.

"Please, God," I whispered, looking up at the ceiling. "Let Tommy be safe."

I got up and took one more look out the window. Paxon was gone, but Lynx wasn't. Knowing I wouldn't get any sleep tonight unless I gave him a piece of my mind, I turned off the lights in the apartment and stomped my way downstairs and across Boylston.

When I passed the corner store, both Rashid and his father waved. I should've stopped to say hello, but I was too angry.

Ready to do battle, I opened the patio's gate and stalked over to him. When my eyes met his, my own pain was reflected in them. All the fire, along with the fight, drifted away.

"Will someone be joining you?" I asked like he had the first night I met him.

"I hope you are," he responded, quoting my exact words.

"You remember. I'm surprised."

"I told you before; I remember everything, Emerson."

"I left London the next day. Not because of you or us or whatever. My father called to tell me that my brother had overdosed."

He leaned forward and rested his elbows on the table. "I'm sorry for your loss."

"Thank you. That was a long time ago."

"Three years," he said.

"Look, Lynx…Lennox…I don't know what to call you…"

"Lynx is fine."

"You didn't let me finish earlier. Tommy and I…Saint, we…"

I stopped talking when it looked like he was ready to get up and leave a second time. Instead, when he reached across the table and took my hand in his, I had to turn away.

"Emerson, please look at me."

A boulder of sadness settled on my chest, and I knew what was coming.

"The night you and I shared was something I've already told you I'll never forget. But that's what it was, one night. While I would dearly love to recreate what I believe you enjoyed as much as I did, I'm here to do a job. I hope you can understand my predicament."

For the briefest of moments, I was sure I was going to cry. Instead, I squared my shoulders. "I'm relieved because, as you know, Tommy is someone who means a lot to me. I'd hate for you to think there was any chance of us 'recreating' that night."

His unwavering eyes bored into mine, and I found myself wishing I could read his mind like he always seemed to read mine.

"It's really late." I stood and pushed my chair under the table.

"Did you want to stay for a drink?" he asked.

"No. I have an early day tomorrow, but thank you."

It was all I could do to keep my head held high, cross Boylston, and rush into my building. Thank God, Lynx didn't offer to walk with me. As soon as I was inside the elevator, the door closed, and I felt it move, I let go. The tears I'd held in all day came streaming out.

It was after one in the morning, and when I was exhausted, I always cried easily, but this was different. This wasn't a tired cry; this was a breaking-heart cry. Which was silly. How could my heart be breaking over a man I thought I'd never see again? Yes, of course I'd thought about him. Fantasized about him. Dreamed about him. But I'd never dreamed I'd see him again.

When my alarm went off at seven, I was still wide awake. I dreaded going into the office today, even though I wasn't sure Lynx would be there. Maybe he had no reason to be, but then Paxon had said there was information they needed from me and now that I knew who they both really were, it would make it easier on all three of us.

I dragged my tired butt into the bathroom, avoiding the mirror until after I got out of the shower. Even then, the person I saw looked as haggard as I imagined I would.

The notion of calling off sick to head down the Cape and spend a couple of days with my parents was a fleeting thought until I remembered that Tommy was missing. No, I had to go into the office, and not only that, I needed to be in top form. I wasn't even close. If there was a bottom form, that's what I was in.

I was still standing in my bathroom in nothing but a towel, staring at my reflection, when I heard a knock at my door. I dropped the towel, grabbed my bathrobe from behind the door, and ran over to check the peephole. I took a deep breath before I stood on my tiptoes, all the while praying Lynx wasn't the one knocking. My prayers were answered when I saw Paxon instead. What was the saying? Be careful what you wish for?

I pulled the sash on my robe tighter and opened the door a crack.

"What are you doing here?" I asked, immediately feeling like a complete shit when I saw he had coffee and bagels from my favorite place. "Sorry," I muttered, opening the door wide enough for him to come inside.

"Lynx is on his way over too," he said, not attempting to hide the fact that he was looking me up and down.

"Give me a minute." I scurried down the hall to my bedroom. "Make yourself at home," I hollered behind me.

I'd pulled on a pair of slacks and was buttoning my blouse when I heard another knock, followed by muted conversation. I slipped on a pair of heels and walked down the hallway to join Paxon and, I assumed, Lynx.

"Hello. Who are you?" I asked the man seated on my sofa.

He stood. "I'm Decker Ashford, ma'am," he said with a Texas drawl.

"Emerson Charles," I responded and then looked at Paxon, who offered no explanation. I readdressed the stranger. "I'm sorry, I know you told me your name, but why are you in my apartment?"

"Decker is part of a team we're working with to locate Saint and Dr. Benjamin," Paxon told me as though he'd suddenly come out of a fog just as there was another knock at my door.

"Would you like to get that?" I snapped at him, feeling annoyed that he hadn't bothered to notify me in advance of the meeting he'd obviously called in my apartment.

"Uh, sure."

I walked over to the kitchen, leaned against the counter, and picked up one of the cups of coffee, not really caring if it was intended for me or not.

When he opened the door, Lynx walked in, looking as sheepish as Paxon should have. "Emerson," he said, nodding at me. I raised an eyebrow and took another sip of coffee.

"I would offer you gentlemen something; however, I was unaware a meeting was taking place in *my home* this morning." I glared at Paxon as I said it. I was less impressed with the coffee and bagels he brought with him now that two other people had arrived.

"Look, I'm sorry," he said, coming closer to me. "I called, but it went straight to voicemail."

Where was my phone? After yesterday—the longest day of my life—I didn't remember the last time I saw it.

"Are we expecting anyone else?" I asked, never dreaming we were until I saw the look on Paxon's face.

"Let's take this over to Saint's apartment," Lynx suggested.

"I'm curious why you didn't meet there in the first place." I was being a bitch—I knew that—but I didn't appreciate being blindsided this way.

Paxon looked at Lynx, but neither spoke.

"Oh, for God's sake," I muttered. I set my coffee on the counter and went in search of my phone. It wasn't on my nightstand or my dresser. I checked my purse, but no luck there either. I folded my arms and tapped my lips with my finger, trying to recall the last time I saw it. When I looked up, Lynx stood in my doorway, holding up his cell phone.

"I just got a message from Stephen. Nora found a mobile on the counter this morning and wondered if it might be yours."

I dropped my arms and fisted my hands. Could this day get any more infuriating? Wait. Forget that thought. As early as it was, I had no business tempting fate.

"Emerson?"

"I heard you," I snapped, not looking at him.

"Would you like me to—"

"No!"

"But you didn't—"

"No. Whatever you're about to offer, my answer is no."

He held up his hands and walked away. I listened for the front door to close, and when it did, I let out the breath I'd been holding.

"I'm doing this for you, Tommy," I shouted into the emptiness of my apartment. "And I shouldn't, because I'm really pissed at you for leaving the way you did, without even talking to me about what happened. Really pissed," I continued to mutter as I kicked off my heels and stomped down the hallway.

"Why?"

"Oh my God, you scared me to death!" I shrieked and brought my hand to my heart when I saw Lynx standing in my kitchen.

"Why are you pissed at him?"

I folded my arms in front of me. "What are you still doing here?"

"I wanted to talk to you…alone."

"Why? We said everything we needed to last night."

Lynx walked closer to me and unfolded my arms. "If we said all we needed to, why are you angry with me?"

I jerked away from him and walked around to the other side of the kitchen island. "I'm angry because three people unexpectedly showed up at my apartment this morning, and not a single one offered an apology for doing so."

He raised an eyebrow.

"Okay, so Paxon apologized, but that doesn't change the fact that I had just gotten out of the shower and wasn't even dressed when he showed up."

"In that case, I'm very sorry I didn't arrive first."

"You can't say things like that, and wipe that smirk off your face."

He came around the island and stood close enough to touch. "What can't I say?"

"Anything remotely suggestive." Before I could move around to the opposite side, he grabbed my wrist.

"What if I can't help myself?"

"*What?* No." I shook my head.

"What if everything I said last night was the stupidest thing I've ever uttered?"

"You can't fucking do this," I swore as he took a step closer to me.

"Why are you angry with Saint?"

"Tommy."

"Why, Emerson?"

"It's none of your business." I tried to turn my wrist out of his grasp, but he held tight.

"Tell me anyway."

I shook my head again. "No."

"You said he knows why. Tell me."

"You said you were here to do a job. That we had one night, and that was all it would ever be."

"You said you were angry with him for leaving the way he did. What did you mean, Emerson?" He cupped my face with his palm "Tell me this. Do you love him?"

I scrunched my eyes and looked up at him. "What?"

"Do you love him?"

"Tommy?"

Lynx nodded.

"I don't understand the question."

"Tell me if you love him."

13

Lynx

I hated how confused she looked, but I couldn't help myself. I had to know whether all was lost, or if after Saint was found and he and I were on equal footing, there was a chance for me to make Emerson mine.

If she loved him, really loved him, I'd do the right thing and walk away. But if she didn't, I'd know it would be worth it to fight for her.

When she talked about Saint for the second time last night, I wanted to get up and leave like I'd done before, but I couldn't without stiffing on the bill for my drinks, not to mention how horribly rude it was the first time I did it.

While I'd been the one to say we'd shared a magical night and there would be no others, hearing her agree felt like a punch to my gut. The woman I'd spent the last three years fantasizing about was within my reach, but I could no longer touch her. I was thankful that I'd kissed her yesterday, and more than once. At the time, I never dreamed it would be the last time I would.

When she'd stood and walked away, I felt as though she was taking my heart with her. I spent the rest of the night wishing I could undo all of it and tell Emerson that I cared enough to fight for her—if it came to that.

"Do you, Emerson? Do you love him? If you do, I'll walk away."

Her eyes searched mine. "And if I don't?"

"If you don't…" Words weren't enough. I grasped her nape and captured her mouth with mine. When she yielded to me, kissed me with a fervor that matched my own, I had my answer.

She didn't use words, but with her lips, she told me that, at the very least, I had a chance. I slid my hand down her spine and cupped her bottom, tilting her pelvis so she could feel how much I wanted her.

"Wait," she gasped, pushing me away. "Paxon and Mr. Ashford are waiting for you."

I closed my eyes and looked up at the ceiling, silently cursing the meeting we were about to have. "Yes. They're waiting for us both."

When we walked into Saint's apartment, three additional men were there, all of whom I'd been briefing earlier when Irish took it upon himself to go directly to Emerson's apartment. It was something I had every intention of discussing with him later.

"This is my brother, Keon," I said to her when he approached.

Emerson shook his outstretched hand. "It's a pleasure to meet you, Keon."

"Most people call me Edge, ma'am." His eyes met mine, and he smirked, giving me something else to discuss later.

"I'm Grinder—uh, Miles Stone." Emerson shook his hand too.

"And I'm Cortez DeLéon. It's a pleasure to meet you." Rile kissed the back of Emerson's hand rather than shake it.

"Are we ready to get down to business?" asked Decker. The man was no-nonsense, something I appreciated a great deal.

"Emerson," Irish said before I had a chance to speak. "As you're aware, the CIA and MI6 have been working jointly undercover here and at IPP over the last few months."

I watched as Emerson processed the information briefed to her. She walked across the room and over to the window.

"These gentlemen," Irish motioned to my brother, Decker, Rile, and Grinder, "were asked to come on board after the CIA received word of a brush pass between one of our agents and Saint."

Irish took a step closer to her. "They're with a private security and intelligence firm. They'll be leading the mission from this point on."

Emerson tapped her lips with her fingertip, something I noticed she did often. "What was the mission?"

"To locate Saint and Dr. Benjamin," Irish answered.

I watched her blue eyes turn a steely gray. "That isn't what I asked. I said, 'What was the mission?' Not what is the mission."

Irish looked to me, and I shook my head. He'd started this by speaking out when he should've deferred to me. He'd dug this hole; he could get himself out of it.

"For the time being, you, Emme, will be working from a remote location, as will I." For the second time, he didn't answer Emerson's question. I could see her anger boiling to the surface. She took a deep breath and exhaled slowly.

"A remote location? Where? Or is that another question you're refusing to answer?"

"Don't be silly, Emme," he said, turning the hole into a grave. "The Boston CIA field office."

Irish cleared his throat as if he was about to speak again. He stopped when Emerson held up one hand.

14

Emerson

Something had been bothering me all night. Tommy and Paxon had shown up nine months ago. Three months later, I was contacted by Dr. Benjamin. Lynx said Tommy was on Benjamin's detail. How could that be so if the agent arrived before the doctor?

There was something they weren't telling me, and Paxon skirting my questions only served to confirm that suspicion. Lynx was no better. He'd paid attention; at any time, he could've responded.

I looked between him and Paxon; this had little to do with the other men in the room. "Gentlemen, until you are prepared to be completely honest with me, there's nothing further for us to discuss."

Paxon approached me. "Emme, you're a target."

"What does that mean?"

"What do you think it means?"

I was seething at his condescending tone, and took several deep breaths in an attempt to not completely lose my shit. I looked over at Lynx, who nodded. Was he encouraging me to continue my line of questioning?

"Are you saying you believe I'm in danger?" I asked Paxon directly.

"I'm sorry, but I do, Emme. Now you understand why I'm suggesting we work from the field office."

Something else occurred to me that made Paxon's staging the meeting at my place this morning reckless on his part. "I want my apartment swept."

Paxon looked confused. "Do you really think that's necessary?"

"Yes. It's necessary." Lynx answered on my behalf. "She also needs a keypad entry installed."

"I'll take care of both," said Decker.

I needed time to think without six sets of eyes studying my every move. "If you don't need me for anything else right now…"

"I'll walk you over," Lynx offered before Paxon could. Much to my relief.

Once we were in the hallway with the door closed, he put his hand on my arm. "Emerson—"

"I need my phone." Whatever he had to say, I wasn't interested in hearing. While I was more concerned with Paxon's behavior, I still believed there were things Lynx was keeping from me too.

"Mario Andretti is on it," he responded, winking.

I smiled despite how hard I was trying not to.

"He should deliver it shortly."

"Thank you."

When he bent his head as though he was about to kiss me, I moved out of reach.

"Please don't," I murmured. So much had happened in the span of twenty-four hours, and my mind was reeling. I needed to sort it all out. Surprisingly, I found myself wishing I could talk to Nora. I couldn't. In fact, I couldn't talk to anyone outside of the man in front of me and the men currently in Tommy's apartment.

"Emerson, if you and Saint…"

I shook my head, wishing he weren't pushing so hard. "What was it you said about me getting together with Nora?"

His eyes scrunched and bored into mine.

"You said I should see how it goes."

"Are you suggesting we do the same?"

"You don't know anything about me, Lynx. We fell into bed without knowing each other's last names."

"What do you propose?"

I shrugged. "Do I really need to spell it out?"

"Are you suggesting I ask you on a date?"

"No, but the first step should be getting better acquainted."

I frowned when he raised and lowered his eyebrows and winked.

"Very well. Emerson," he sighed. "Would you join me for dinner this evening?"

"I'll have to take a rain check. I'd like to get some rest."

He leaned forward and kissed my forehead. "I'll be down the hall if you need anything."

It wasn't long before I heard another knock at my door. When I looked through the peephole, I saw Lynx's driver on the other side and opened it.

"Your phone, ma'am," he said, handing it to me.

"Thank you…I'm sorry, I don't know your name."

"Mario, ma'am."

"That's funny."

He cocked his head in a way that meant maybe it wasn't funny after all. "Your name really is Mario, isn't it?"

"Yes, ma'am."

"By any chance, is your last name Andretti?"

"Um, no, ma'am, it's Smith."

"Seriously? Mario *Smith*?" I was making this worse, not better. "Wait here, Mr. Smith." I grabbed my bag and handed him two folded twenties. "This is for bringing me my phone."

"That isn't necessary, ma'am. Mr. Edgemon already paid me."

"Are you his driver exclusively?"

He shook his head.

"Hmm." I had an idea brewing and tapped my finger on my bottom lip. "Are you driving for Mr. Edgemon this afternoon?"

"No, ma'am."

"Would you be up for a drive down the Cape?"

He nodded, and his eyes lit up, probably at the prospect of a hefty payday.

"One condition, though."

"Name it."

"You have to drive within the speed limit."

This time he smiled. "I promise."

I pulled him into my apartment by the arm. "Wait here."

"Um…I'm double-parked, ma'am," Mario called after me when I walked toward my bedroom to call my parents.

"Go downstairs and tell Mr. Bridges you're waiting for me. I'll be down in a jiffy."

I made two calls. One to my office to let them know I'd be taking a few days off, and then to my parents to let them know I'd be visiting. I'd just finished packing my bag when I heard yet another knock at my door.

I checked the peephole, and instead of Lynx or Mario checking to see what was taking me so long, Paxon stood on the other side.

"Are you going somewhere?" he asked, eyeing the suitcase next to me.

"To see my parents."

"When will you be back?" he asked.

"I'm not sure, Paxon."

"Can I give you a lift?"

"No, um, Lynx's driver is taking me."

"Huh. Okay, well, can I walk you downstairs?" he asked, picking up my bag.

I thanked him and locked my apartment door behind us. Once we were in the elevator, Paxon set my bag on the floor.

"Emme…I just want you to know…Lynx told me about you and Saint."

"Yes, well…" I stammered, not knowing exactly where he was going with this, especially when he cleared his throat and took a step closer to me.

"I realize that this might be coming out of left field for you, but to be honest, once this mission was over, I planned to ask you out myself."

I bit my tongue to make sure my mouth wasn't hanging open. In the last several months, I'd had fewer dates than I could count on one hand—and dinners with Tommy didn't qualify. Those weren't dates. Well, until the last one, but I hadn't known it was a date, not until he kissed me when he walked me to my apartment. Even then, it wasn't a date. It was dinner, followed by an unexpected kiss.

I looked up at Paxon, who seemed to be waiting for me to say something. I could ask why he had this sudden interest, but that might come across as rude. I put my finger on my lip, trying to think of something that might not offend him. "Uh, that's very nice…" I said as we exited the elevator.

He handed the driver my bag, and I was about to get in the car when Paxon put his hand on my arm.

"Wait. I want you to know that when his boss leaves your heart in pieces, there's someone who cares enough to help you put it back together."

Before he could say anything else, I got into the waiting car and closed the door behind me. His boss?

Whose boss? Mario's boss? I closed my eyes and rested my head against the seat. Paxon had to mean Lynx.

But why did Paxon think Lynx was going to leave my heart in…what was it he said? Pieces.

"Mario?"

"Yes, ma'am?"

"You aren't at all attracted to me, right?"

"Um…you're very pretty, ma'am, but…I'm married."

"Thank God," I muttered. "Oh! I have one stop to make on our way."

After our stop at MIT, the rest of the hour-and-a-half drive down the Cape was uneventful. Once I'd given Mario my parents' address, neither of us said another word, and I was grateful for the solitude.

I smiled when the car pulled into the driveway and I saw my mother and father sitting on the second-story deck. My mother stood and came to the railing while my father walked down the stairs that led from the deck to where we were parked.

"Aren't you a sight for sore eyes?" my dad said as I fell into his embrace. "What's this?" he asked when he saw tears in my eyes.

"I don't know why I don't visit more often." I looked up to where my mother stood. "I miss you both so much."

My dad put his arm around my shoulders. "You're here now. That's all that matters." He looked at my head. "What happened?"

"Minor cut," I muttered, paying Mario and thanking him after he'd taken my bags out of the trunk. He nodded, and before I could say another word, he was in the car, pulling away.

"Interesting fellow," my dad muttered.

"You don't know the half of it."

He chuckled and led me to the front door, where my mother stood waiting. She held out her arms, and I walked into them like I had with my dad. Once again, I felt myself tearing up.

"I'm so glad you're here," she said, stroking my hair.

"I missed you so much, Mom. I'm sorry it's been so long."

"What's this?" she said, just like my dad had, and then looked at my head.

"You two are so much alike. Minor cut," I said, pointing to where the bandage covered the staples.

My mother shook her head and took my hand. "Come in and eat. You're getting far too skinny."

After lunch, Dad went for a walk on the beach, leaving Mom and I alone in the kitchen.

"Why are you really here, Emme?" she asked.

I put my head in my hands, wondering how so many people could figure out what I was thinking and feeling without my saying a word about it. First Tommy, then Lynx, and now my mother.

"I needed a break."

She shook her head. "Try again."

"I've been working such long hours, and quite frankly, I'm beginning to burn out."

My mother kept her gaze steady on me while she drummed her fingers on the table.

"All right," I sighed, knowing how relentless she could be. "Three years ago, when I was in London for that conference…you know…"

"Yes, I know," she said, motioning for me to go on.

Thankful that it wasn't necessary to mention it was when my brother overdosed, I took a deep breath. "I met someone."

"And?"

"We didn't exactly stay in touch."

My mother smiled and tilted her head. "Emme…too much time has passed for you to tell me you're pregnant, so get to it. What's happened?"

"I ran into him yesterday. At my building, and, well, later at the office. And then I hit my head and needed staples, so he called his friend. It was actually his cousin, who was at MIT for a conference. Later we went to his house for dinner, and I met his wife—his cousin's wife that is—who's really such a lovely person. Someone I hope I can be friends with. And—"

"Stop!" My mother held up one hand. "Repeat the part where you ran into him yesterday at your building. Then you can tell me about the staples."

I covered my face with my hands, wishing I could avoid talking about Lynx. Talking about him required thinking about him, and that wasn't something I wanted to do.

"Emerson?"

"I'm trying to decide where to start."

15

Lynx

When I returned to Saint's apartment, Decker was huddled with my brother, Rile, and Grinder. I didn't see Irish, and that was fine with me.

"Anything I can do?" I asked.

Decker shook his head. "I'll let you know when we're ready for you."

As Z had said, we were going off the books for this one. We'd hired a team, and I needed to let them do their job. "I'm going for a walk," I muttered, not that it appeared anyone had heard me.

I went across the street to the corner market, where I found Rashid's father behind the counter like I had yesterday. Had that truly only been twenty-four hours ago? It seemed so much longer.

"Another chai for Emme?" he asked.

"Not today, thanks. But I'd like one."

He grunted something I couldn't understand, came around the counter, and walked to the rear of the store.

"Make it caffeinated," I hollered after him.

When he returned a few minutes later, it was with a paper cup instead of the ceramic one that he'd given me for Emerson. That was likely still in Saint's apartment; I made a mental note to return it later.

I paid the man and picked up a circular on my way out. There was a park just north, and it was the perfect place for me to take a few minutes to think through the events of the last twenty-four hours.

Saint was one of my men, and if he were here in front of me, I'd be tempted to fire him. He'd always been a loose cannon, as the saying went, and Z had made it clear he expected me to rein him in. I hadn't, and that was part of the reason Saint was now missing.

There were times I considered the man more of an asset than a fellow agent. I'd even made the suggestion to Z that we offer him a reduced role. Z had told me at the time to wait and see how this particular mission went. I suppose we both had our answer.

Getting involved with Emerson, someone he'd been tasked with turning into an asset, had been reckless. But was what I was doing any less so? Did the fact she and I had shared one passionate night three years ago, somehow give credence to my pursuit of her being any different?

What I needed more than anything was to sort out how I really felt about her. I'd asked myself before if when I saw her again, she'd live up to my memory. Had she? I couldn't say for certain. I was so wrapped up in her for the last twenty-four hours that all I could think about was her in my bed, naked and warm, as I buried myself inside the best pussy I'd ever had. Was it really as magical as I remembered it being?

Maybe I should let her be tonight and go out on the pull. Perhaps getting laid would be the best thing I could do to let go of this obsession I had with Dr. Charles.

I sat up against the trunk of a tree and skimmed the weekly entertainment guide I'd picked up on my way out of Rashid's father's store. It seemed that every bar and pub advertisement was aimed at a crowd far younger than me. So much for going out on the pull.

I closed my eyes, content to feel the soft breeze on my face as the tree shaded me from the ungodly heat of the city.

I'd give just about anything to have this mission over and take a holiday, perhaps even staying on in the States for a time. To what end, though? When it was over, Saint would return, and then I'd learn exactly what his relationship with Emerson truly was. If my fears were confirmed, I'd much rather be in England.

My mobile buzzed, jarring me awake. I must've drifted off, but I had no idea for how long.

"Ready for me?" I asked when I saw the call was from Decker.

"Lynx, are you aware Dr. Charles is on her way out of town?"

"What? No, I left her at her apartment," I looked at my watch, "less than an hour ago."

"Where are you now?"

"On my way."

I ran across the street, took the stairs to Saint's floor rather than wait for the lift, and entered my code. When I walked in, Decker and Irish were in the midst of a heated discussion.

"Lynx's driver took her," I heard Irish say.

"Took her where?" I asked.

"To visit her parents."

"You didn't know about this?" Decker asked.

"Of course I didn't." I already had my mobile out and was ringing Mario.

"He's your driver, how did you not know?" Irish asked.

I ignored him and listened as the call went to voice-mail. "What did he look like?"

Irish described the man along with the car while I rang another of my agents, who was also here in Boston.

"Hi," she answered.

"I need transport arranged from Boston to Cape Cod."

"Understood. I'll meet you downstairs in twenty."

I walked out of the main living area and into Saint's bedroom, trying to rein in my temper as I did.

"What's your plan?" asked Decker, standing in the doorway.

I ran my hand through my hair and walked over to the window. "I'd like to wring her neck before I bring her back."

"You might not want to bring Emerson back right away."

I turned my head and studied him. "Why not?"

He handed me an envelope.

"What's this?"

"Background on Emerson's father."

I opened the envelope, skimmed the first page of the report, and then looked up at Decker, who raised a brow.

My mind reeled as I processed what I'd just read. Why was I learning of this just now? I answered my own question easily enough—because knowing previously had been above my paygrade.

I didn't bother asking Decker how he'd amassed this information—it was accepted throughout the intelligence community that the man was able to find the proverbial needle in the haystack when neither MI6 or the CIA could.

"Thanks for this," I said before sliding the document back in the envelope.

"I'll brief you on what else we know before you leave."

I nodded and followed him out to the main room where he laid out the intelligence they'd received confirming Saint and Dr. Benjamin had been in Hong Kong, but from there, their trail had gone cold.

"We'll be in contact when we know more," he said.

My mobile buzzed with a text message. "My transport is waiting." I stood and shook Decker's hand and then walked over to my brother and put my hand on his shoulder. "Godspeed, Keon."

He repeated my motion. "Godspeed, Lennox."

It was something we always did whenever we were together and one or both of us were leaving. It began shortly after our parents' death.

As I turned to leave, my eyes met Irish's. I didn't like what I saw in them, but I didn't have the time or inclination to deal with that now. He followed me out to the lift.

"I hardly need an escort," I snapped at him.

"I'm going with you."

When the lift arrived, I stepped inside, turned around, and stood in the threshold, barring his entry. "You're doing nothing of the kind."

"This is the CIA's mission as much as it is yours."

The level of my temper was equal to what it had been when I was informed Emerson left without my consult or permission. I didn't owe the man in front of me any kind of explanation, and it was unlike me to parlay information when it wasn't necessary. However, this agent was becoming a problem, and I needed to set him straight.

"The CIA's initial mission was to convert Dr. Charles into an asset in the same way MI6 intended to. Given that the mission was aborted upon the disappearance of one of our assets along with one of our agents, you," I looked at him pointedly, "are no longer needed."

I stepped back, allowing the lift's doors to close.

"Thanks for getting here so quickly," I said, getting into the vehicle and closing the door behind me. "Do you know where you're going?"

"Initially," the agent, code name Angel, answered.

I would ask what she meant, but I was still reeling from the combination of Emerson's reckless action along with Irish's insubordination. I would ring Copeland, but before I did so, I needed to temper my frustration. I let my head fall against the seat and closed my eyes. I had a great deal to process on a drive that should take a minimum of ninety minutes.

I opened my eyes when Angel brought the vehicle to a stop and cut the engine.

"This will be quicker," she said, pointing to the helipad with a waiting copter.

Even more surprising than our unexpected mode of transport, was that Angel climbed into the cockpit, handed me a headset, and sat in the pilot's seat. I shook my head. Teagon Engel, aka Angel, was one of those MI6 agents who, every time I saw her, had acquired yet another skill. "When did you get your pilot's license?"

"Just helly for now, mate, but I'm working on the other."

"Congratulations, Angel. I'm proud of you."

She smiled, and her cheeks flushed.

"What?" she asked when I continued staring.

"Nothing." What I couldn't tell her, not that she'd care, was that her sweet cheeks did absolutely nothing for me. Emerson's, it seemed, were it for me.

"Is this a touch-and-go retrieval, or are you sticking around?" Angel asked through the headset once we were in the air.

"I'll be staying, at least for a time."

"With Charlie?"

My eyes opened wide at her use of the nickname. "Do you know her?"

"No, but Saint talked about her quite a lot."

I was not prone to motion sickness, but suddenly, I felt nauseous.

"What does he say?"

"You can't quote me on this."

I held up a couple of fingers like some kind of half-assed pledge.

"He was pretty pissed the last time I saw him. We both were ten sheets gone, actually."

"What did he say, Angel?"

She raised a brow. "Why so anxious?"

I looked away. "Just tell me."

"Now I'm wondering whether I should."

Probably wouldn't be wise to strangle the pilot, considering I didn't know how to fly one of these things, but I was close.

"Angel, please."

Her eyes scrunched in confusion, but then she shrugged. "Remember, he was absolutely smashed."

I nodded.

"He said, and I quote, 'someday I'm going to marry that girl.'"

My nausea was now full-fledged. "Was he serious?"

"He was drunk, Lynx. I mentioned that three or four times."

"I know, but was he serious?"

Angel shrugged again. "Kind of seemed that way to me."

16

Emerson

My parents and I were sitting at the dining table, finishing our lunch, when we heard a loud whir. Jumping up, my mother and I ran to one window while my father headed to the back door.

With wide eyes, I watched as a helicopter landed on the lawn next to our house.

"Um…could it be someone you know?" I asked as my mother and I followed my dad out onto the back porch.

He shook his head.

A door opened, and I watched Lynx climb out. "Never mind," I mumbled. "He's here for me." I continued to watch as he stalked in my direction and the helicopter took off.

"What are you doing here?" I asked when we stood practically toe-to-toe.

"I might ask the same of you."

I took a step back. "I'm visiting my parents."

"Without a bloody word as to your intentions?"

"Not that I need to explain myself, but I did tell Paxon."

"Oh, you told *Paxon.* It didn't occur to you to consult with me before gallivanting off for the second time with little regard to your safety?"

I didn't care for his raised voice any more than I did the way he was speaking to me. *"For the second time?"* I shouted back.

"First, you sneaked out of Saint's apartment when my back was turned. This time, you left the building as soon as you were out of my sight."

"Are you serious? You can't be—"

"I'm Rick Charles," my father said, inserting himself into our heated conversation. "This is my wife, Rebecca."

"Lennox Edgemon," Lynx said, extending his hand to my mother first and then my father. "It's a pleasure to meet you, ma'am, sir." He smiled at them, but when he turned back to me, he scowled.

"Is this the young man from London?" asked my mother, feigning innocence, but I was onto her.

"Yes," I seethed, my hands in fists at my sides.

"Come," my father said, escorting Lynx inside while I stood frozen where I was.

"Close your mouth, Emme," my mother scolded before following.

"Your home is lovely," I heard Lynx say when I came in and slammed the door behind me.

"Emme will give you a tour while I make us something to eat," said my mom, ignoring my bad manners and motioning us out of her way. I knew better than to remind her that we'd finished lunch less than thirty minutes ago.

"Can I get anyone a drink?" my dad asked, motioning for us to follow him out onto the porch.

"I could use one," I said, raising my hand and glaring at Lynx.

"I'm making street tacos," my mother hollered at us.

"Street tacos?" I mouthed to my father, who shrugged.

"Margaritas, then?" my dad asked.

"Add a little extra tequila to mine, please."

My father rolled his eyes. "Show your friend around, Emme. I'll deliver your cocktails in a few minutes."

Without thinking, I took Lynx by the hand and led him down the steps and out onto the beach.

I dropped his hand, spun around, and folded my arms. "Why are you here?"

"You left without permission."

"Permission?" I seethed.

Lynx stepped closer and got right in my face. "You are in danger, Emerson, and it is my responsibility to keep you safe. You left without a word after I'd expressly said that if you needed anything, I was down the hall."

I took a step back and put my hands on my hips. "First, you insinuate yourself into my life after a simple cut on my head. Then, you insist you're personally responsible for my safety when you aren't even sure I'm in danger."

"I hardly insinuated myself into your life. You were concussed, and I stayed to make sure your condition didn't worsen. Like then, I'm here now in order to ensure your safety. I have no intention of letting anything happen to you, Emerson, whether you like it or not."

"Why?" He was close enough that if I moved even a fraction of an inch, our lips would touch.

"Because."

I couldn't hide my smile. "Because why?"

"Because I said so."

Our stare-off continued until I turned away and sat in one of the Adirondack chairs that overlooked the bay. He sat in another.

"Why are you really here, Lynx?"

He took a long time to answer. "I was worried," he eventually said, almost too quietly for me to hear.

"Am I really in danger?"

He turned toward me, his green eyes piercing mine. "Whether I'm certain you are or not, I cannot take the risk."

"What's going to happen?"

"The men you met this morning will locate Saint and Dr. Benjamin by any means necessary."

I loved that he knew what I was asking even though a minute ago we'd been arguing. "What can I do?"

"Give those doing the job the time and space to do it."

"How can you be so calm?"

"I've been where they are, and I know firsthand how badly things can go when someone interferes."

"I don't want to go back to Boston with you."

"You don't have to."

"When is he returning?" I asked.

Lynx tilted his head. "Who?"

"The helicopter pilot."

"She won't return until she hears from me."

"I suppose that was sexist of me, but what I'm about to say is even worse."

"What's that?"

"Is she pretty?"

"Here we are," said my father, approaching with our drinks.

Lynx brought his glass to mine. "You have nothing to worry about, Emerson, no one on earth is as pretty as you are."

—:—

Before I knew it, it was after nine o'clock, and the four of us were still seated at the dining room table. My father entertained us with stories about his time with the state department while my mother kept the food and drinks flowing. When I finished my third margarita, I placed a napkin over my glass.

"Mom, stop," I whined when she moved it and filled my glass anyway.

"Lynx told me you aren't going back to the city tonight, so you can have another."

"What about you?" I asked him, pointing to the time and wondering if he was feeling as tipsy as I was. Actually, I was flat-out drunk.

"He's staying," my mother answered for him while pouring him another round.

I looked over at my father, who shrugged.

"Oh my God," I mumbled, covering my face with my hands. "I'm sorry about this."

Lynx put his hand on my arm. "Don't be."

When I looked into his eyes, all I could think about was dragging him upstairs and into my bedroom. I didn't even care that my parents would be in the same house. I wanted him to do what he'd done three years ago, and fuck me senseless.

He leaned forward so his mouth was close to my ear. "I'll go, if that's what you want," he whispered.

I leaned into him without thinking. "No, that isn't what I want at all."

"Leave all this, I'll clean up in the morning," I heard my mother say as she pulled my dad out of his chair. "Come on, Rick, time for bed."

"But you just poured me another drink, why am I going to bed?" We could hear my father's protest as she led him up the stairs.

"I made up the room downstairs for you," my mom shouted from the top of the stairs. "Good night! Sweet dreams!"

I put my head back in my hands. "I feel like a teen-ager, except in an alternate universe where my parents are encouraging me to have sex in the downstairs guest room."

"Really? They're encouraging us to have sex?" Lynx raised his eyebrows. "I *love* your parents." He stood and held his hand out to me.

"Lynx…"

"Come with me," he murmured, pulling me from my chair, but more gently than my mom had with my dad.

Since he didn't know where the stairs were that led to the lower level of the house, I was interested to see where he'd go. We went out to the screened-in side of the back porch and over to the daybed that hung by ropes from the ceiling.

"Looks sturdy enough," he said, sitting down and pulling me with him.

"When my dad put it up, he made my brother and all his friends get on it to prove to my mom it was safe for the two of them to sleep on."

"Do they?"

I shrugged. "I have no idea. I would if I were them."

"Let's do it, then." Lynx scooted up the bed so his head rested on the pillow and held out his hand for me to join him.

"Lynx…what…I mean…what are we doing?"

"Just lie next to me."

I scooted up like he had, and when he held his arms open, I snuggled up to him.

"Lynx?"

"Shh. Let's just enjoy the peacefulness of this place for a bit."

I loved the night sounds of Cape Cod Bay. Crickets and cicadas chirped, and every once in a while, an owl would hoot.

This house had been in our family for generations. My great-great-grandparents built it, and then each of their heirs had added their own touches to it. Growing up, I'd been the envy of all my friends who had to spend their summers in the heat and humidity of the city. I was never popular until a new batch of kids found out about the house down the Cape.

"What are you thinking about?" Lynx asked.

I shifted to roll my shoulders. "Spending summers here when I was growing up."

"Why does that make you tense?"

I smiled even though he couldn't see me. "Is it that obvious?"

"Your body speaks to me."

"It does, does it?"

"It has since the moment we met."

Whether it was true or a line, I loved the way it sounded.

"Tell me the good part of spending summers here."

"So much. Watching the sunrise and sunsets from Nobscusset Point, all the lighthouses, eating littlenecks and cherrystones all summer. Laughing to the point my stomach hurt all the time."

"Sounds wonderful. Tell me more."

"Four-wheeling on Nauset Beach, lobster instead of turkey on Thanksgiving. That isn't a summer memory, but it's still a good one." I realized that I was smiling and the tension had left my shoulders. "Dad used to take us out on the boat on the Fourth of July because he said the best view was from the water. Ricky would always bring friends along…Ricky was my brother."

"Your father's namesake."

"He was actually Richard Jefferson Charles the fifth. So several namesakes."

"Sounds like nobility."

"We hail from a long line of New Englanders. This house has been in our family for four generations. I guess that makes us Cape Codder nobility. What about you? Any noblemen in your family?"

"Would you hold it against me if I said there weren't?"

"Of course not."

He sighed. "There isn't much to tell, really."

I raised my head so I could see Lynx's face. "Do you have any brothers or sisters other than Keon?"

"He's my sole sibling."

Given his entire demeanor changed, I hesitated to ask anything else. If he didn't want to talk about his family, I would be the last one to push. I almost never talked about my brother.

"When I was eighteen, my parents were killed in an automobile accident. Keon was with them."

"I'm so sorry."

"He spent several weeks in hospital. Enough that he had to repeat year eight."

"So he was thirteen at the time of the accident?"

Lynx nodded. "My plans to go to university were temporarily dashed…"

"You took care of him."

"Yes, I did, not that the bloody wanker appreciated it." Lynx smiled.

"What makes you say that?"

"I understand he's taking up permanent residence in Texas."

"Texas?"

"My little brother has always fancied himself a bit of a cowboy. Never mind that he'd only ridden English until he was in his mid-twenties." He shook his head.

"What made you go SIS?"

"At the time, a degree wasn't required—still isn't necessarily, but more and more applicants have one. I was twenty-three when I finally sent Keon off, and had little idea what I wanted to do with my life. SIS ended up being a good fit for me." Lynx stroked my cheek with his fingertip. "I did eventually earn my degree. More than one, actually."

I wanted to ask what they were, but given my educational background, I didn't want Lynx to think I was being competitive.

"That night we spent together…I want you to know, it meant something to me."

"Lynx, you don't have to—"

He studied my face. "It meant something, Emerson."

It meant something to me too, and if my brother hadn't died, I probably would've wanted to see Lynx again, not that the desire would've been reciprocated.

"I lied to you," he blurted.

Oh, God, was he married? Or worse? Although what could be worse? "When?"

"When I told you I didn't look for you."

"Lynx, really, you don't have to make me feel better about it. I was a grown up then, well sort of, but I am a grown up now."

"I went down to the front desk, and they told me you'd checked out. I have to admit I was quite worried. One of the conference organizers was standing nearby and overheard me. I suppose the look of utter devastation on my face was reason enough for her to take pity on me."

"You're serious?"

"Yes, I am. She told me you'd withdrawn due to a family emergency. I wanted to wring her neck when she gave me your contact information. Major security and privacy breach, that was."

"But you didn't contact me."

"No, once I found out about your brother's passing, I decided it would be best if I didn't."

"So…you knew?"

"Yes, Emerson. I knew. And while I could've used my position with MI6 to find out more, my conscience prevented me from doing so. I assumed that if you'd wanted me to know how to find you, you would've left a note or a message or something."

I wasn't sure what to say. Part of me was too shocked to believe him, but why would he make up such an elaborate story just to make me feel better?

"You never told me why you left before sunrise, Emerson."

And I didn't want to now. I felt just as embarrassed as I had three years ago. "You were my first…my only… one-night stand. I wasn't sure of the…etiquette."

"I see. So you chose the walk of shame rather than allowing me to order you a proper breakfast."

Lynx was smiling, but in my mind, it had worked out for the best. "I wasn't in my room very long before my father called."

He nodded as if he understood.

"I'm sorry you wasted a trip out here. The helicopter ride probably cost a fortune."

"I've no idea about the cost. However, you are in my arms, Emerson, I'd hardly call that a waste."

"Lynx…"

"Emerson…"

"Wait," I said when he brought his lips to mine and was about to kiss me.

"Please, I beg you, don't say another word about Saint."

"I have to."

He groaned, rolled to his back, and covered his eyes with his forearm. "What?"

"More than once, you alluded to, even mentioned, my relationship with Tommy."

"Yes?" he grunted.

"I wasn't in a relationship with him. We weren't seeing each other."

He rose up, turned to his side, and rested his head on his hand. "He said you were."

"Pretty sure I'd know."

I stood, and Lynx sat all the way up, looking out at the bay. "You said when he kissed you…"

"Once, Lynx. Tommy kissed me once."

17

Lynx

"Once?"

Why had Saint told me he and Emerson were seeing each other if they'd only kissed once? It didn't make sense. What Angel told me didn't make sense either, unless I'd somehow misunderstood.

I rolled from the bed and wrapped my arm around Emerson's waist, turning her so I could look into her eyes. She wouldn't lie; she had no reason to. And even if she had reason, something told me the woman in my arms would never be dishonest.

My mind raced with the number of times Emerson had referred to Tommy, and whether she'd said anything that would've confirmed what Saint told me. Other than telling me how stunned she was when he'd kissed her, I couldn't recall anything else.

"I'm not saying that I expect us to pick up where we left off." Even in the dim light, I could see her cheeks flush the prettiest pink with her words. "I just wanted you to know that Tommy and I weren't…together."

I cupped the back of her neck with my hand and brought my forehead to hers. "You said something about not picking up where we left off, but I think we should."

"We should?"

I nodded. "If I recall correctly, I was about to kiss you." I captured her lips with mine and kissed her like I'd wanted to every minute since the last time I had.

Knowing there was nothing between her and Saint, made me want to rip through every other barrier there was between us—namely clothing.

I nuzzled her neck, breathing in the scent of her. It was the same as I remembered, only now there was an added layer of a day spent by the sea. She smelled divine, and soon instead of merely nuzzling the soft skin of her graceful neck, I kissed it.

When she shuddered in my arms, I wanted to make it happen again and again—all night long.

I captured her lips with mine and devoured her mouth in a frenzy of unmitigated desire. I couldn't rein myself in even if I wanted to.

"Say it," she whispered.

"Say what, my darling?"

"Say what you said that night, in the elevator."

I reached around her and cupped her gorgeous, heart-shaped arse with my hands, lifting her so her legs wrapped around me. I looked into her eyes and said the words she asked me to.

"Emerson, I'm going to fuck you senseless."

She brought her lips to mine and kissed me so hard I could taste the tangy copper hint of blood, but I didn't care. It only drove me to devour her more.

I lined my cock up with her pussy and rubbed against her. Her shorts were so thin, I could feel her wetness and her heat. She unwound her legs from my waist, and I eased her onto the daybed.

"Lynx," she whispered, pulling me down with her. But I couldn't take her. Not yet.

"Come," I said.

When she stood, I grabbed the blanket from the daybed and took her hand, pulling her toward the beach.

"This way," she said, and I followed her instead. When she stopped, I laid the blanket on the sand and then pulled her into my arms.

I kissed her again, deeper, harder, pulling her body as close to mine as I could. When she tried to pull away from me, I wove my fingers in her hair.

"Ouch!" she yelped, covering my hand with hers.

"Oh, God, I'm so sorry."

"Kiss me again and make it all better," she said, bringing her lips back to mine.

"I have a better idea." I unfastened the button on her shorts and knelt in front of her, pulling them along with her panties down with me until they were around her knees and I was on mine.

"Thank fucking God," I murmured, piercing her slit with the hard tip of my tongue. "Every time I closed my eyes, I imagined you this way. Bare, like you were that night."

I rubbed my face against her bare pussy and then leaned back on my heels and looked up into her beautiful blue eyes. "Take off your t-shirt."

She pulled it over her head and tossed it on the blanket.

"Now your bra."

She reached around and unfastened it, letting it slip from her arms. I knelt up, burying my face between her tits, teasing each nipple between my fingers. I pulled until she gasped and then buried my mouth in her pussy. Her fingers threaded in my hair, holding me to her clit. I sucked hard and thrust two fingers into her drenched heat. Her essence coated my face as she screamed out her release.

Her knees gave, and I caught her in my arms, spilling us both onto the blanket.

"You are really good at that," she moaned, looking up at me with the most gorgeous smile. I leaned forward and kissed her lips, then her cheek, down her neck, and to the nipples I'd brutalized with my fingers.

"Oh, no," she said when I reached her belly button.

"Emerson," I groaned when she pushed me onto my back, unfastened my trousers, reached inside, and wrapped her hand around my girth. Her thumb brushed against the tip, spreading the moisture she found there around the crown.

"I can't wait," I said, moving her hand away as I took off the rest of my clothes. I pulled out my wallet, praying that there was a condom tucked inside. "Thank God," I muttered, ripping the package open with my teeth. I sheathed myself, spread her legs, and lined myself up at her entrance.

"Please," she whispered, and it almost undid me. I thrust inside of her, burying myself as deep as I could.

"Fuck," I moaned, holding myself above her. "Just like I remembered." I steeled myself against coming too soon and began moving again, slowly. "So tight… so hot…so incredible." I sped up my thrusts and captured her lips with mine.

When her nails dug into my back, I moved harder, faster, fucking her so deep. "So right," I said out loud, slamming into her hard, again and again, until I roared my release.

I thought back to our one night together, remembering how we took pleasure in each other's bodies again and again.

I removed the condom, tied it closed, and dropped it near my clothes. I wrapped my arm around her and drew her close. "Emerson," I said as though it were a prayer.

Her head rested on my chest, and she trailed her fingertips over my skin. All I could think about was how badly I wanted to be inside of her again, especially when her hand drifted lower. "I need you again," I told her when her hand stroked my already steel-hard cock.

"Lynx…I…you know…"

I bent my neck so I could see her face. "What do I know?"

"I am on birth control."

I smiled, in fact, I laughed, remembering how insatiable we both were that night. "I can't get enough of you," I growled, pulling her so she was on top of me.

"I can't get enough of you either."

"Take what you need, Emerson," I said, staring into her eyes as she lowered herself until her warmth wrapped around me. I recalled wondering if her pussy would be as magical as I remembered, and it wasn't. It was better. It was heaven.

When the sun peeked over the horizon, we dressed, and I carried my beautiful, sleepy Emerson back to the house, lowering her body onto the daybed. She rolled over, and I covered her with the blanket.

I sat next to her, stroking her hair, wishing I didn't have to think about what might happen later today, or tomorrow, or the day after that.

One day soon, I'd get the word that it was time for me to leave. I'd be part of the team that would go into wherever Saint and Dr. Benjamin were being held, extract them, and then bring them home.

Home wasn't here in America; it was in England. Not just their home, but mine too.

I kissed the cheek of my sleeping princess and then eased my body off the bed.

"Good morning," Emerson's father said, startling me when I walked through the door from the back porch into the kitchen.

"Good morning," I responded, shielding my eyes when he turned on the light.

"You and I should have a chat, young man," he said, motioning for me to follow.

—:—

"What are you doing here?" asked Irish when I opened the door to Saint's apartment.

"Why are you still here?" I replied.

"HQ for this op."

He was baiting me, and I was in no mood nor did I have time to engage. I walked down the hallway to retrieve my bag and saw Decker Ashford set up in Saint's office.

"Are they off?" I asked, confirming my instructions that Rile, Grinder, and my brother return to England until further notice. Decker and I would follow in two days' time. If we needed to deploy, we would be twelve thousand kilometers closer from there than here.

"Affirmative."

When I returned, Irish was waiting for me. "You headed back down the Cape?"

It wasn't any of his bloody business, and I resented the hell out of him for asking. I was about through the door when I heard him speak again.

"Where's Emme?"

I pulled the door closed behind me.

—:—

"Thanks for seeing us, Ambassador. This is Lennox Edgemon, aka Lynx, MI6."

"What's this ambassador shit? How the hell are you, Matrix?" I watched as the U.S. Ambassador to China stood, embraced Emerson's father, and patted him on the back.

"I'm Terry Stevens. My friends call me Buster." I shook the ambassador's outstretched hand. He walked over to a cabinet, opened the doors, and slid out what looked like a well-outfitted bar. He removed the stopper from one of the decanters and poured three glasses.

"Thank you, sir," I said when he handed one to me and one to Emerson's father.

The ambassador raised his glass. "Here's to nukin' those fuckers, or to be more politically correct— may the bold, the true, the gallant prevail." The man downed the contents in one shot and slammed the glass on his desk.

"Have a seat, and let's get down to business. When Matrix here called me last night about this, I had my people reach out to some of our assets."

"I appreciate that, sir."

"I'm afraid the news isn't good. Our sources have confirmed that two British citizens matching the description of your missing agent and his asset were arrested in Hong Kong. They weren't alone. Two of our people were with them. I haven't been able to confirm if they're still there or if they've been transported to Beijing."

My mind raced as I processed the ambassador's words. Other than knowing Saint and Dr. Benjamin had been arrested, we were no closer to knowing where they actually were. And now, instead of two, we'd be going in after four.

"You've heard of Operation Fox Hunt?" the ambassador asked me with scrunched eyes.

"Yes, sir."

He went on. "Their aim is to pursue Chinese citizens who have fled here after *allegedly* committing crimes. There's no extradition treaty between our country or yours with China, and neither of us has been in the mood to cooperate with Beijing."

I knew that the Chinese government had deployed undercover agents not just to the U.K. and the States, but to other countries within the EU as well as Canada.

One of their tactics was to harass family members living outside of China, in order to coerce targets to return.

"You know what they're gonna do to 'em if we extradite 'em, don't ya?"

"Yes, sir, I do."

The longer Ambassador Stevens spoke, the angrier I got with Dr. Benjamin. Assuming he was the one who set this in motion, he'd played right into Beijing's hands, and the price the U.S. and the U.K. would have to pay was a steep one. So steep, I doubted they'd do it.

"I expect that I'll be hearing from Beijing sometime in the next forty-eight hours as will my counterpart in the U.K. They'll tell us there's an investigation pending on whatever charge they've trumped up, and then they'll tell us what will make their investigation go away."

I already knew. There were three highly sought-after dissidents who had been given asylum in the U.K., and four in the U.S., all of whom China had been after for several years on espionage charges.

"What can I do, Buster?" Rick asked.

"Reach out to Jinyan."

I watched Emerson's father raise his eyebrows.

"Don't give me that shit, Matrix. You're in contact with him, I know you are." The ambassador turned to me. "Will you excuse us, young man?"

"Of course." I stood and walked out. Before the door closed behind me, I heard the ambassador tell me not to go very far.

What I really needed to do was call Z, who likely knew at least some of this already, but certainly not that Ambassador Stevens had gotten involved, or the role Rick Charles was playing in this.

I'd been waiting less than five minutes when Emerson's father came out and closed the door behind him.

"Let's go," he said, motioning for me to follow.

"Sir?" I asked when we walked out and the same SUV that met us on the tarmac was waiting at the curb.

"I'll explain once we're on the plane."

I nodded and followed. What the hell else could I do?

—:—

When the plane landed at the private airfield near Logan, Rick's vehicle was waiting on the tarmac like the SUV had been when we arrived in Washington. It wasn't until we'd almost arrived at the house that he pulled the car over.

"I don't know about you, but I could use a drink."

"I should really—"

He held up his hand. "I'll be inside when you're finished talking to Z."

I could hear my boss laughing when he answered my call. "I've got to hand it to you, Lynx. I don't know how you did it, but somehow you got an audience with not just Buster Stevens but Matrix Charles as well. You might just get knighted for this one—that's if you manage to get Dr. Benjamin the hell out of China without giving up the Chinese dissidents."

And Saint, I thought to myself, but knew better than to say it out loud. At this point, it was more likely Z would rather leave him there to rot.

"My plan was to return to London."

"Are you daft? I know agents who would give their right arm to be in your position. You'll stay put until you get further orders from me."

18

Emerson

Give your parents my thanks.

No matter how many times I picked up the note and read it, no other words magically appeared.

"Good morning, honey. Where's your friend?"

I folded the piece of paper Lynx had left on the daybed next to me and shoved it in my pocket. "He had to leave. He said to thank you and Dad."

"I'm sorry he couldn't stay longer. It looked like you enjoyed his company and vice versa. Can I get you more coffee?"

Nodding, I picked up my cup and handed it to her.

"He's the young man from London, right?"

"You sound like Grandma Charles right now."

"I suppose I do," she said, pulling out the chair next to me. "You don't look happy."

"Pretty sure we covered that yesterday, Mom. Right before a helicopter landed on your lawn."

"I need to ask you something."

Oh, God. Here we go. "Mom, please. I'm not in the mood to talk."

She put her hand on mine, and I knew there was no way I'd get out of this conversation. "Okay, forget my question, just tell me what happened with Lynx."

"He left before sunrise." Little did she know how apropos that was. Something else occurred to me. "Where's Dad?" He was always the first up; my mother loved to sleep in.

"He went into the city."

"Why? When?"

"Earlier."

Two and two suddenly added up to four. "You are fucking kidding me."

"Emerson Jane."

I stalked over to the kitchen sink and tossed my coffee down the drain. "Are you serious right now?"

"You know he can help."

"Why did you ask me where Lynx was if you already knew?"

"Emerson…Jane…please…sit…down."

I hated the way she enunciated every word like she used to when I was a kid in trouble. I was twenty-eight fucking years old.

"Do you want some more coffee?" I asked, resorting to civility in the hope she'd calm down.

"Yes, and pour yourself some more too."

No *please*. That wasn't good. I did as she asked, sat down, and folded my arms on the table. "Go ahead."

"When your father got up this morning, Lynx was up too. He offered to drive him to Boston."

I'd surmised that, but I doubted now was the best time to be a smart ass.

"Tell me about Lynx."

"I already told you I don't want to have this conversation."

"Do it anyway."

"Things aren't as simple as they may appear."

My mom reached over and put her hand on mine. "We've got all day, Emerson."

"Lynx is an MI6 agent."

She nodded as though she already knew that.

"He's here because two of the people I've been working with on Chinese grand strategy have disappeared. Well, really only one that I work with. The other is my neighbor. Although, I think that maybe he's been undercover too. Well, I don't think; I actually know that he's with MI6, but that doesn't change the fact that they've both disappeared. And evidently, Lynx thinks I'm in danger, even though—"

"*Emerson!*" my mother gasped, holding up one hand. *"Slow down."*

I took a deep breath. "Okay, so the MI6 agent who's missing…his name is Niven St. Thomas, I call him Tommy. Anyway, the last time I saw him, we went to dinner, and then after dinner, he kissed me."

"Does he know about Lynx?"

"No, because I didn't know about him either."

"What do you mean?"

"I told you yesterday that I met him three years ago, and then he showed up at my building."

"Forgive me if this is all a bit much for my addled brain to remember."

I rolled my eyes. "Lynx showed up in Boston yesterday. Prior to that, I didn't know anything other than his first name." I felt my cheeks flush and waited for my mother to look shocked. *Or something.* Instead, she motioned for me to get on with it.

"Tommy has been gone for over two weeks."

"Okay. I've got it. Before he left, how did you and this other guy leave things?"

I laughed out loud. We all knew who my mom was backing in this horse race.

"I freaked out."

"What does that mean?"

"I didn't expect him to kiss me."

"Then what happened?"

"He left."

"Tommy left? So he kissed you, and now he's been gone for two weeks. Did he call?"

I shook my head. "Did he call? Did you not understand the part where I said he's missing?"

"He's gone. There's no reason you can't move on with Lynx."

"It isn't that simple, not to mention that sounds a little heartless."

"What's stopping you?"

"Because, other than having sex with him for one night three years ago, and the fact that he's here now to find his missing agent, well, and the doctor who's missing too…wait. What were we talking about?"

My mother shook her head. "You and Lynx."

"There is no me and Lynx, although there kind of is." I studied my mom's face, wondering if I should go on.

"What happened?" she asked, reaching out to cover my hand with hers.

"We had sex. Last night."

"Then why would you say there is no you and Lynx?"

"Because he left." I dug the note out of my pocket and handed it to her. "Show me where it says he wants to see me again."

—:—

I'd been sitting on the beach, throwing rocks into the water for God knew how long when my mother sat down beside me.

"I've news."

"What?"

"Your father is on his way home."

"I was beginning to think he took Lynx all the way to London."

"Yes, well, not quite that far. They did go to Washington."

I put my head in my hands. "Oh my God. What did Dad do?"

"You'll have to ask him yourself. Here he is now."

I looked behind me, ready to give him the third degree, but he wasn't alone. Lynx was with him, and by the look on his face, it was obvious he'd already anticipated I wouldn't be happy to see him. I stood and stalked down the beach away from them.

"Emerson," I heard my mother call after me, but I was already yards gone, brushing the sand off my butt.

I'd begged my dad not to interfere when I went to work for MIT. Begged him, and he'd promised me he wouldn't. Granted, two men had disappeared, but still, he'd usurped me, and I didn't like it.

"Emerson, wait," I heard Lynx call after me, but I kept walking. I knew he'd catch up with me in a matter of seconds, but I sure as hell wasn't going to just let him—so I started to run.

I was right. Mere moments later, he was right behind me.

"Stop!" he shouted.

I did, but I didn't turn around to look at him when I said, "I thanked my parents for you. Was there anything else?"

He came around and stood in front of me. "There were things I needed to take care of. I didn't plan to come back."

"So leave." Instead of standing there not knowing what to do with my hands, I sat down on the sand. I expected Lynx would too, but he didn't. He stood behind me and put his hands on my shoulders.

"What I'm about to tell you isn't likely to sit well."

"Say it and get it over with."

"I'll be staying on here indefinitely."

"Wow. I'm so happy to hear that," I said with zero inflection. When I tried to stand, I knew why he had his hands on my shoulders. To hold me in place.

"Hear me out."

He sat beside me; I still hadn't looked at him and didn't plan to. The man was just too damn good-looking. If he smiled, I'd probably melt into a puddle, and I didn't want to melt. I wanted to stay mad at the way he'd left this morning, essentially without a word.

"Dr. Benjamin and Saint were arrested in Hong Kong."

"Oh my God." I put my head in my hands, half with worry and half ashamed that I'd been so wrapped up in being mad at a man who was simply trying to save lives. "What now?"

"Our governments will work to get them released."

"What about your brother and the other men? What are they doing?"

"We're attacking from both sides. One way or another, we'll get them out of China."

I looked out at the water. "Then what?"

"What do you mean?"

"You'll return to England."

It took him a while to answer. "Yes, Emerson."

I stood and walked in the opposite direction, past my parents' house and farther down the beach. I didn't turn around and look for Lynx; I already knew he wasn't following me.

"What do you mean I can't come back?" Why had I called Paxon in the first place?

"What did Lynx tell you about the brush pass?"

I held the phone away from my ear, seriously contemplating disconnecting the call. "Paxon," I seethed. "I am in no mood for games. If there's something I need to know, just…fucking…*tell me!*"

"Okay, you don't have to yell. Saint's message contained a warning."

I was ready to scream. Literally scream. If there weren't hordes of families on the beach wherever I looked, I would have. "What…was…the…warning?"

"Essentially, it said to keep you safe."

I rolled my eyes, ready to pull my hair out. "That isn't a warning."

"Look, you need to talk to Lynx. If you don't want to talk to him, talk to your dad."

"My dad? What the hell does my dad have to do with this?" Thirty sets of eyeballs landed their shocked gaze on me. Yes, I'd just yelled, and if half of those eyeballs didn't belong to children, I would've flipped them all off. Instead, I walked in the opposite direction of the water, toward the parking lot.

"Hey, Emme," I heard someone shout at me. I waved in the direction of the voice and kept going.

"Are you going to answer me?"

"I can't. Talk to Lynx."

Beep, beep, beep. The bastard hung up on me.

When I walked into my parents' house, my mom, dad, and Lynx were all seated at the dining room table. I continued past them and was halfway up the stairs when I heard my father ask me to join them.

"Please," he said, standing at the bottom of the stairs.

Paxon's words replayed in my head. *"You need to talk to Lynx. If you don't want to talk to him, talk to your dad."*

I didn't understand what my father had to do with this. He'd retired from the state department three years ago, right after my brother died. Before he had, he'd been the Undersecretary for Arms Control and International Security Affairs. It wasn't a stretch to think he would have insight into China, but how much could he possibly have after all this time? And then to further confuse me, I was one of the leading policy writers for Chinese Grand Strategy. If he did have insight, why in the world hadn't he ever discussed it with me? Maybe because I had specifically asked him not to interfere in my work, but still, it wasn't just national security at risk.

"Emme," he said again, walking up to where I stood.

I sat down on the stair, and when he sat beside me, I rested my head on his shoulder. "I feel like you're hiding things from me."

When my dad took a deep breath and let it out slowly, he confirmed my suspicions.

"There are things you don't know about my time at the state department. Partially because you had no reason to, until now, and partially because most of it I wasn't able to tell you."

I sat up straight and folded my arms. "I have a feeling I don't want to know."

"I think you can piece it together."

"Who did you really work for?"

My father sighed. "I was with State, but I also consulted with the NSA."

"On?"

"Cryptography."

"His code name is Matrix," said Lynx, who I hadn't seen standing on the steps below us.

When his eyes and my father's met, I felt sick to my stomach. It was bad enough that I was learning something I'd never known about my dad in front of a man who was essentially a stranger to me—a stranger who had fucked me senseless just last night—but that Lynx knew more about him than I did, infuriated me all over again.

I stood, walked down the stairs, and got right in his face. "How long have you known?"

His eyes scrunched. Was he realizing how betrayed I felt? "Since yesterday," he answered.

"Why?"

He cocked his head.

"This is need-to-know. Why did you need to know?"

"Let's sit," said my father, who now stood on the stair right above us.

"How much of this did you know?" I asked my mother as I pulled out the chair next to her.

"Leave your mother out of this," my father warned.

"Why? She's seated at the table, is she not?"

"*Emerson.*"

I remembered when Lynx had said my name the same way my father just did. It freaked me out then and now.

"I can speak for myself, Rick," said my mother, resting her hand on my arm. "I knew who your father worked for and what he did. I knew none of the specifics. Even if I had, I doubt I would've understood any of it. It's you and your father who have the genius-level IQs."

"May I?" Lynx asked my dad.

"Go ahead."

He faced me, but I didn't do the same.

"Your father and I traveled to Washington today and had a meeting with the U.S. Ambassador to China."

"Buster?" my mother asked my father, who smiled and nodded.

"The ambassador was able to confirm that Saint and Dr. Benjamin, along with two CIA operatives, were arrested in Hong Kong. We believe negotiations will soon begin, but what Beijing is likely to ask for, may be out of the realm of possibility."

"A swap," I murmured. If there was anyone at this table who had a clear picture of China's tactics, it was me. I lived and breathed it on a daily basis. I was one of the people—one of a handful—who disseminated highly classified information provided by organizations like State and the NSA, and mapped out strategy. With China, my primary objective was to head off their ability to seize the title of one true superpower from the United States. They were close, and it was my job to figure out how to stop it from happening.

If it came to what Lynx was suggesting, there was no way we could negotiate with their demands. None. Doing so would go against everything the United States stood for. If the U.K. was asking us to, I'd be the first to recommend saying no. Yes, it meant losing four good men to a Chinese prison, or worse, but what would happen if we caved was exponentially more horrific.

"I hope you're right about your team being able to get Saint and Dr. Benjamin, along with the other two, out of China," I mumbled.

Lynx nodded. "I am."

19

Lynx

It was fascinating to watch Emerson process information. I'd seen the look on her face before when she questioned Irish and me about MI6's and the CIA's involvement at IPP. It was almost as though an alternate personality took over when she went into analytical mode. She was lightning quick and needed little explanation, spitting out questions faster than AI could generate algorithms.

Pride shone brightly on her father's face, and rightly so. His daughter was fucking brilliant.

My reaction? My cock was rock hard. Never before had I wanted her as much as I did at this moment. Part of me wanted to toss her over my shoulder and carry her off to my lair, the other wanted to bow down at her feet and beg her attention.

It had taken me far longer to come to the same conclusions she had, and I'd had it essentially spelled out for me. The only hope that Saint and Benjamin would make it out of China alive, was black ops.

"What about Jinyan?" I asked Emerson's father. "Are you in contact with him?"

Emerson's eyes opened wide, and Rick nodded.

"And?" I asked.

"You and I need to stay out of it."

I understood. Rick would put the man capable of giving the Invincible team the information they needed for a successful extraction, in direct contact with them. Jinyan was a code name for a Chinese intelligence officer who had direct ties to the highest level of U.S. government. In other words, he was an invaluable double-agent whose identity needed to be protected at any and all costs. The less Emerson's father and I knew about what he told the Invincible team, the better it would be for everyone seated at this table.

Emerson stood. "I need to take a walk."

She didn't invite me along, but I was on her heels anyway.

By the time she stopped walking and looked over at me, we were beyond the place on the beach where I'd caught up with her earlier.

"What in the hell was Benjamin thinking? Has he no idea what he's done?" she asked.

Benjamin's agenda was to protect the United Kingdom. Emerson understood that stopping China from gaining further advances in the areas that would define a country as a superpower, was a global concern.

She sat down on the sand and dug her fingers into its warmth.

"Tommy and I didn't meet by chance, did we?"

"No."

"Did you have anything to do with it? My meeting him?"

"I did."

She shook her head. "I'm an idiot."

"You're not."

"When it comes to men, I am. You set me up. Why, Lynx?"

"I told you before, I had no idea that you, the Emerson of our encounter three years ago, were Dr. Charles."

"Like I said, idiot when it comes to men."

I reached over and took her hand. "Not with me."

She looked down at where my thumb caressed her palm. "With you especially."

"Why?"

The longer she stared into my eyes, the more hers filled with tears. "Because with you, I'd want more."

The moment of truth had arrived. It was up to me to tell the beautiful woman next to me whether I could offer more. I couldn't lie. The truth was, I didn't know whether I could or not.

As I watched Emerson walk away, I called the only person I could think of who might understand what I was going through.

"Lennox, Nora and I were just talking about you. How's the patient?"

"Listen, Stephen," I said, cutting to the chase. "I need a favor."

"Name it."

"Are you on duty this weekend?"

"As a matter of fact, I'm off."

"Can you and Nora, and the kids of course, manage a weekend down the Cape?"

20

Emerson

"Hi, Daddy," I said, sitting down in the Adirondack chair next to him.

"Where's Lynx?"

I pointed down the beach. "Out there somewhere."

"He seems like a decent guy, Emme."

"Decent. Right. The kind of guy you'd buy a used car from."

My dad laughed and then looked at me in a way I couldn't stand. "Don't pity me, Dad."

"Pity you? It's him I pity."

"Why?"

"Because you, Emerson Jane, are formidable."

"I don't want to face him in battle."

"They say love is a battlefield."

I sat up straighter. "They do?"

"No, probably not, but I did have a huge crush on Pat Benatar when that song came out."

"You and mom are both weird."

"She used to look a lot like her."

"What in the name of God are you talking about?"

My dad laughed. "You sound just like her."

"Who? Mom or Pat Benatar?"

When he answered, "Both," I got up and went inside only to find Lynx in the kitchen, talking to my mother.

"Emme, there you are. I was just telling Lynx that there's no reason for his cousin and family to stay in a hotel, we have plenty of room here."

Yes, we did have plenty of room, eight bedrooms in fact, in this monstrosity of a house. "There's room," I muttered, turning to go upstairs.

Actually, there was no one I could think of that I wanted to talk to more than Nora. I wouldn't admit that to Lynx, though.

I was in my room with the door closed when I realized I should've asked when they'd be arriving.

—:—

"This place is fabulous," Nora said the next day as we sat on the back porch, watching Lynx, Stephen, Brian, and the twins play on the sand closer to the water. My mom and dad were out there too, and I swear they were sending me telepathic messages about how much they wanted grandchildren. Maybe they could just adopt Stephen and Nora's kids. It would come with a nice house.

"Oh my God, is that a bed?" she asked, pointing to the screened-in porch where Lynx and I had begun and ended our night. It had only been two days, but it felt like a different lifetime.

"Sure is."

"I'd love to be able to sleep outside in the summer," she said wistfully. "Lynx said this house has been in your family for generations."

I told her the same thing I'd told him about how each generation added their own special something to the house.

"What will you add?" she asked.

"Me?"

"It'll be yours one day."

I hadn't thought about that. My father had been an only child, and while I wasn't, since my brother was gone, I guess technically, I was. I bent my neck and looked up at the house that always seemed too grand for our family.

Along with its eight bedrooms, it had nine bathrooms and indoor and outdoor kitchens. Besides the daybed, Dad had added a saltwater pool and a large pool house. That had been at my mother's request.

The house sat on five sloping acres fronting Cape Cod Bay and had its own salt pond. Almost every room afforded a spectacular view, either of the water or the rolling marshes; even the master bathroom's whirlpool tub—something else my dad had added—looked out on the bay.

I sighed, wondering what would come of it once my parents passed away. There was no way I'd be able to handle the upkeep involved in an old house like this, and the likelihood of me marrying someone who could, given my track record, was a flat zero. It made me too sad to think about.

"Are you okay?" Nora asked, reaching over to take my hand in a gesture that spoke of a friendship older than a few days.

"I've a lot on my mind."

She followed my gaze to where Lynx sat on the sand, looking our way.

"He adores you."

"He doesn't know me."

"That," she said, pointing at him with no apology, "is not the look of a man who doesn't know you."

Lynx smiled and then fell backward into the sand when one of the little girls climbed all over him.

"And he's a good sport," she added.

"His life is in England."

Nora was quiet for so long I thought maybe she hadn't heard me.

"When Stephen and I first started…seeing each other… he was a resident at the hospital where I worked." She stopped talking and waved at her husband when he blew her a kiss.

"The way we started out was…unconventional, but the important part of what I want to tell you is, when we first got involved, he'd only planned to be in the States a few more months. In fact, while we were seeing each other, he returned to England for a job interview. I was heartbroken, but had convinced myself it was for the best."

I knew where she was going with this, and my heart wanted me to stop her. It wasn't the same. Lynx and I had sex. That was it. There was never a time we were "seeing each other." We'd had a couple of nights of sex and nothing else.

"I should backtrack. When I met Stephen, Brian and I were living on our own. My husband, Brian's father, was killed in a car accident when our son was six years old."

"I'm so sorry."

"Thanks. Anyway, I don't know if you know this, but I'm older than Stephen. Five years older."

"It doesn't appear to matter."

"It did to me, especially in the beginning." She cocked her head and smiled. "I'm taking too long to get to the point."

"You're fine."

"Stephen was renting a room from me, and…one thing led to another and…we started having sex. It was far more complicated than that, but that's what it was. We wrote each other these letters…" She smiled and shook her head. "That isn't important. What is important is that I convinced myself that Stephen and I would never have a conventional relationship. He was a playboy-doctor, and I was a mom. And look at us now."

"Yes, look at you now. What happened?"

"We fell in love, and then Stephen realized he wanted to be with me more than he wanted to live the rest of his life in England."

"Lynx is with MI6," I blurted and then realized I probably shouldn't have.

"It's okay. I know."

"He has to return to England, and my life is here."

"Does it have to be?"

Did it? God, why was I even thinking about it? "We don't even know each other," I reiterated, maybe more for myself than her.

"But you both want to."

21

Lynx

"How'd you know Nora was…the one?"

"Besides wanting to spend every day buried—"

I nodded my head toward Brian.

"Besides knowing I couldn't live without her?"

"How long did it take you to realize it?"

"I went to England to settle a few things, and after I did, all I could think about was returning to the States as quickly as I could."

I looked up at the house where Stephen's wife sat talking to Emerson, and a life flashed before my eyes.

This could be us. Emerson and me, spending summers here with our wee ones, as happy together as Stephen and Nora were.

But how? I thought about my younger brother and how crazy I believed he was to give up his position with MI5 to go out on his own. Not to mention, Z Alexander had made it perfectly clear that he considered me next in line for the chief position. While Z wasn't a young man, he wasn't exactly old either. He could continue in his role for many years.

"She says I don't know her."

"Do you?"

"I feel as though I've known her all my life."

"Then convince her of it."

I looked up at Nora and then again at Stephen. The love the two so obviously felt for one another made my chest hurt. Could I have that? Truly?

"Did you have to convince Nora?"

"To the point I thought I'd go mad. But I realized I had to prove it to her, not convince her. She had to trust that I loved not just her, but Brian too."

I saw the boy's eyes meet Stephen's.

"Yeah, I love you, okay?"

Brian smiled, shook his head, and refocused his attention on filling molded plastic shapes to build his sisters a sandcastle.

"I don't know," I murmured.

"Until you do, you bloody well won't be able to get her to trust you. You shouldn't even try."

That night, as we all sat around the dinner table, I watched Emerson laugh so hard she wrapped her arms around her stomach. I remembered her saying that it was one of her happiest memories of spending her childhood here. With everything that had happened over the course of the last three days, I hadn't thought it would be possible for her to laugh like she was; I was so glad she was able to.

"Oh, Rick, I love this song," exclaimed her mother. "Come dance with me."

I found myself humming along to the song I knew well.

Moments later, Stephen held his hand out to Nora, and the two joined Emerson's parents, each couple swaying to the music as they held each other close. I longed to feel Emerson in my arms. In fact, they ached with the want of it. When I looked over at her, I saw the same need written on her face.

I stood and held out my hand, but she didn't take it. Was I wrong? Had I misinterpreted what I thought I saw on her face? Evidently, I had. I dropped my hand and walked out onto the back porch and then down to the beach. I kept walking until I reached the deserted stretch where Emerson and I had had sex two nights ago, wondering what in the hell I was playing at.

The woman was a challenge. That was the entirety of it. I woke that morning three years ago, and she was gone. If she hadn't been, things would've turned out vastly different. I didn't love Emerson like Stephen loved Nora. For me, it was about the conquest. It always had been. My job gave me the perfect excuse to walk away when I was ready to. As an MI6 agent, I traveled the world, never knowing how long I'd be in any one place.

My home—which wasn't much of one—was a residency suite in the same hotel where I'd met Emerson three years ago. I didn't have one at the time, but I stayed there often enough that it made sense to.

I'd said I'd give anything to feel Emerson's naked body beneath mine one more time, and I had. But now, what? Was I ready to say goodbye to her like I did to every other woman I'd ever been with? Saint and I weren't so different.

I laid back on the sand and looked up at the cloudless sky, imagining where we'd be now if she'd only taken my hand.

—:—

I rolled to my back and put the pillow over my head. It sounded like a herd of elephants was traipsing on the floor above me. I reached for my mobile and checked the time. "Bloody hell," I muttered. It was seven in the morning.

I wondered if Emerson was awake yet. Was she an early riser, or did she like to sleep in? The first night I'd spent with her, she was up before dawn, but was that indicative of her usual habits?

While I would normally roll over and at least try to return to sleep—particularly on a Sunday at this hour—curiosity got the better of me.

I'd slept in the nude; my shorts and shirt were tossed on the floor somewhere. I got up and donned both before making my way to the lavatory.

After splashing water on my face and cleaning my teeth, I crept upstairs and eased open the door that led to the hallway off the kitchen. From there, I had a clear picture of the elephants. Stephen was crawling about the floor, as was Brian, gently bumping the two twins with their heads as they raced around them. Emerson was seated at the dining table with her arms once again wrapped around her stomach as tears of laughter ran down her cheeks.

If things were somehow different, if she were mine, I'd make it my life's mission to make her laugh that hard at least once a day.

I closed the door behind me, nearly slamming it. Things were not different, and they never would be. I'd leave this place when Z gave me the word, and travel on to some other part of the world, for some other mission, on behalf of MI6. I found myself resenting the job I had so dearly loved from the day I was sworn to duty.

I was about to walk back down the stairs when the door behind me swung open. "Breakfast is ready," Emerson announced. "Don't expect much. I made it, but Nora did supervise. After we eat, we're going for a hike, if you'd like to join us."

"Are you always so chipper first thing in the morning?"

"First thing? It's almost half-past seven." The door closed again, and I had my answer. My Emerson was definitely an early riser. Considering at least part of my body was too, that might work out very well for me.

"I feel almost guilty," I heard her say to Nora when I joined them in the kitchen.

"Why do you feel guilty?" I asked, looking around for a tea kettle but settling on a cup of coffee as easier.

Emerson walked over and refilled her cup.

"Cream or sugar?" she asked.

"Both, if you have it. So, why?"

"You know…Dr. Benjamin and Tommy," she whispered.

"Dr. Benjamin knew full well the danger he was putting himself in when he decided to take on the entirety of the Chinese government by way of Hong Kong. And Saint signed up for duty just as I did. Can you imagine if everyone stopped living their life whenever there was some kind of crisis? The world would be a bloody sad place."

She cocked her head. "Good morning to you too, Lynx."

I took a sip of my doctored-up coffee and let my gaze linger on hers. "I can be a bit off-putting first thing in the morning."

"Good to know."

"Not you, though, you're a right morning person, yes?"

"It's not something I'm ashamed of."

"Nor should you be."

"We're going on a hike. Are you joining us?"

I looked down the length of Emerson, decked out in her short shorts and a t-shirt that every so often moved enough so I could see the bare skin of her tummy. Up the highest mountain, down the lowest valley—I would follow wherever she led.

When my eyes returned to her face, her cheeks were the most delightful shade of pink. Again, in that alternate universe Emerson had mentioned the other day, the one in which her parents were encouraging us to have sex, it would be my goal not just to make her giggle, but to blush as often as I could as well.

After the morning hike, that everyone went on, including the twin girls, carried on the backs of Stephen and myself, the lot of us took a dip in the saltwater pool, played on the beach, and partook in far too much food and drink. When we reached the end of our day, I was sad it had come so quickly, and wished Stephen and his family could stay longer.

"When are you and Nora meeting up again?" I asked once they'd left.

Emerson blushed that lovely shade of pink. "As soon as I'm back in Boston, although depending on how long I end up staying here, she may try to come down again."

"Need I remind you—"

"Yes, Lynx, you told me so."

Rick and Rebecca called an early night for themselves, and I wondered if Emerson would want to do the same.

"I'm going to watch a movie," she said and then added, "if you'd like to join me."

"I would."

She bit her bottom lip. "I'm kind of particular."

"Go on." I smiled inwardly, anxious to hear what her particularities were.

"I prefer older movies. Romantic comedies. Is that okay?"

"My favorite as well."

She smiled, the first I'd seen since my cousin and his family left. "They are not. Anyway, I'm up to 1958. The choices are *Vertigo, Gigi, Separate Tables, South Pacific,* and *Indiscreet.*"

"Hmm. Tough choices, but I'll go with *Indiscreet.*"

"Clark Gable and Ingrid Bergman. Two of my favorites."

I watched as Emerson queued the movie. There was so much about her I could easily become addicted to. The blush of her cheeks, her smile, the soft skin on her neck, her long legs, and what I remembered was between them.

"Popcorn? It's one thing I know how to make, and with a pan I'm allowed to use."

"I'd love some popcorn, but there are pans you *aren't* allowed to use?"

"Don't feel too badly for me. My dad isn't allowed to use them either."

"Why not?"

"My mom is a cooking freak, especially when we're here, although she's not much better at home. What was it you said about missions going badly when other people interfere? She feels the same way about food."

When Emerson returned a few minutes later with a bowl of near-orgasmic buttery goodness, I considered proposing on the spot. "If this is what you can do with popcorn, I'd love to see what else you know how to make." Seriously, this was the best popcorn I'd ever had.

"I'm pretty good with trifle, but that doesn't require cooking."

Imaging whipped cream, strawberries, ladyfingers, and Emerson together, I had to shift where I held the popcorn bowl. When she dipped her hand in, I considered moving it the next time she made a reach.

"What about you? Do you cook?"

Having raised my brother from the age of fifteen, I'd learned to cook quite well actually. "I'd show you if you could convince your mother to let me use her pans."

"That's a stretch, but maybe when we're in Boston."

Her face heated, and she quickly looked away.

"I think I would enjoy cooking with you, Emerson."

She smiled. "You might want to rethink the 'with' part."

"What else do you make other than popcorn and trifle?"

"Mostly things that come in a box, which are truly disgusting for the most part. I can heat things up in the microwave, though."

Twenty minutes into the movie, Emerson was sound asleep, reminding me what she'd said about being a good sleeper that first day when she cut her head and we were in Saint's apartment.

I eased my arm around her, loving it when she snuggled against me. I rested my head against hers, breathing her in, and for the second time, a life flashed before my eyes.

After a day spent in the sun and sand, our children in bed, Emerson and I would cuddle up and watch another year's best romantic comedies. She'd fall asleep in my arms, but when I carried her upstairs to bed, she'd wake, and we'd spend the hours until dawn ravaging one another's bodies.

I'd spend my days making her blush, making her giggle, cooking dinner while she did brilliant things to save the world.

Was it insane that these were now my fantasies? I'd spent three years dreaming about fucking her senseless, and now I dreamed of settling down and raising children with her.

Did the fact that I could see these things so clearly mean I was ready to manifest them into reality? Did I even have that option? It wasn't entirely up to me. Emerson was half of this equation, and I had no idea how she felt.

22

Emerson

When I opened my eyes, the sun was just peeking over the horizon. Lynx was beside me, and we were on the daybed on the back porch. I vaguely remembered falling asleep while we watched a movie, but that was all. Had Lynx carried me out here?

I did what I'd wanted to do the morning I woke up in his hotel room three years ago, and studied his sleeping form. I'd never woken up next to Tommy, but I doubted even he would look as beautiful as Lynx did.

His dark eyelashes were impossibly long, and it looked like he had a smile on his face. As though he sensed me staring, his eyes opened.

"Good morning," he said with a sexy rasp to his voice.

"Were you dreaming?"

When he smiled, he looked like I'd just caught him being naughty. "I was."

"About?"

"Are you sure you want to know?"

I nodded, and he shifted his body so his steel-hard erection poked into me. He cupped my cheek with his palm and looked into my eyes. "I dreamed about a lot of things last night."

"All the same subject?"

"Yes."

I scrunched my eyes.

"You," he said.

"Sex with me."

"Not necessarily, although there was a lot of that."

I was intrigued. "What else?"

"Watching movies, making popcorn, spending the day on the beach."

"Like we did yesterday." I looked up at the sky. "I'm going to admit something I probably shouldn't."

He propped his head on his bent arm. "Yeah?"

"Don't get too excited…it isn't what you think."

"I read your thoughts, not the other way around."

I laughed. "I had a good time yesterday. I liked you being here. With me. With my family. Having Stephen and Nora and their family here. It was nice."

It was actually a lot more than nice. I didn't want to think about him leaving and how quiet, lonely, and boring it would be once he was gone.

"It was nice," he murmured.

"It was like in the movies. The boy and girl meet over summer vacation, and then at the end of it, they go their separate ways, but they'll always have the memory of that one magical time together." I needed to change the subject; I'd put myself on the verge of tears.

"When you used to spend summers here as a child, what were your daydreams? When you closed your eyes, how did you imagine your life would turn out?"

"That's quite a question, but not at all the way it did."

"How is it different?"

"I never imagined that I'd graduate from high school when I was fifteen. I sure didn't imagine that I'd go to Stanford, all the way on the other side of the country."

"What was that like? How'd you manage?"

"My parents rented a house, and my mom lived there the whole time I was enrolled. Dad came out when he could. Ricky…my brother…" Did I really want to talk about this? It was the beginning of the end. "He stayed in Boston because it was his senior year."

Lynx looked into my eyes. "And then what?"

"He was a football player. The first game of the season, he got hurt and had to have surgery. Mom flew out right away so she could be there. I don't remember where Dad was. Anyway, she made it before they took him in to operate. His recovery was rough. He was in a lot of pain, but instead of being with him, Mom flew back to take care of me."

"That's when he began taking fentanyl."

I nodded and closed my eyes. "If Mom had been with him, she would've monitored how much he was taking."

"Maybe."

"No, she would've. It's how she is."

"The way it played out wasn't your fault."

I shook my head. It was, because it didn't end there. My parents spent as much time as they could in California with me. They'd tried to talk my brother into applying for colleges there, but he refused. He wanted to stay in Massachusetts near his friends.

He'd dropped out of college after the first year, and that's when they realized there was something very wrong. His first stint in rehab later that year was in a facility less than an hour from Stanford. I sat up and turned my back to him.

"It wasn't your fault, Emerson," Lynx repeated.

I tried to stand, but he wrapped his arm around my waist.

"It wasn't your fault," he said a third time.

I bent at the waist, with his arm still encircling it, and cried.

"Let it out," he soothed as sobs racked my body. This certainly wasn't the first time I'd cried over my brother, but it was the first time anyone other than my parents held me while I did.

I tried to stop, but I was too far gone, so I did as he said and let it out. Lynx stayed behind me, whispering all the while that it was okay, I was okay, and it wasn't my fault that my brother overdosed.

I'd heard the words so many times when counseling was a regular part of my life. No matter how many times I heard them, it didn't make them true.

If I hadn't gone to Stanford, things would've turned out entirely differently. Maybe if we'd been at the game that night, he wouldn't have gotten injured.

"I need to use the bathroom," I said, moving his arm so I could stand. I went into the house and upstairs. When I came back down, Lynx was sitting at the table, talking to my dad.

"Rough morning?" my father asked when I joined them. He held his hand out to me.

"Thinking about Ricky."

"It's my fault," said Lynx. "I asked Emerson about her childhood, and one thing led to another."

"Nothing is anyone's fault. In fact, it's a word we don't use in our house. If we did, we'd never be able to move on with our lives. Instead of losing one precious life, we'd lose four, because no one in our family would truly be living."

It wasn't the first time my father had said something like that. It reminded me of how yesterday morning, Lynx had asked me to consider how sad it would be if everyone stopped living their life whenever there was some kind of crisis.

Sometimes, though, it was impossible not to get mired down in the sadness of it all.

Without Stephen and Nora at the house, the rest of the day was quiet. Too quiet. When my mother suggested a change of scenery would do us good, I agreed wholeheartedly.

We spent the afternoon in town, shopping, and then having drinks and dinner at one of my favorite bayside restaurants. When Lynx reached over and took my hand under the table, it felt like the most natural thing in the world. And then, when we returned to the house, we fell asleep on the daybed like we had the night before.

When I woke the next morning, I knew I couldn't spend another day like yesterday. It was going to be far too difficult when Lynx left as it was. The more I got used to him being around, doing things like holding my hand during dinner, the more heartbroken I'd be when it was time for both of us to return to our lives back in the real world.

23

Lynx

"I feel like it's time I returned to work," Emerson said when I opened my eyes and found her sitting next to me with a cup of coffee in hand.

"Your magical summer holiday is at an end?"

Emerson bit her bottom lip; it was her worry tell. "At the very minimum, I should check in."

When she went inside, I rang Decker.

"I was wondering when I'd hear from you."

"Haven't you been in communication with Z?"

"Of course I have, asshole. I'm just giving you shit. What's up?"

"Emerson is talking about returning to the office."

"Is there any reason she shouldn't?"

Not any I could think of. As long as she understood that she would still have security detail, whether it was me personally or someone else, like Angel, for example.

"What about Warrick? What was he still doing there the other day?" It occurred to me that I'd never called Copeland to discuss having Irish reassigned.

"I'm glad you brought that up."

"Go on."

"Something felt off, so I put a tail on him yesterday. You'll never guess where he went—MIT."

"Why?"

"I don't know, but he was there all day."

"Perhaps Emerson's return is in order."

I went inside and found her father in the kitchen.

"Anything I should know about?" he asked.

"I believe Emerson and I may return to Boston soon."

He nodded and poured himself a cup of coffee. "Want some?" he asked.

"Sure." It wasn't as though this was the first time I'd opted for it over tea in the morning. There were certainly times that neither had been an option, given where I was in the world and the level of danger of whatever mission I'd been assigned.

After I'd added the requisite amount of cream and sugar, Rick motioned for me to follow him outside.

"Let's take a walk."

I fought against the feeling I was being led to a gallows of sorts.

"After we lost Ricky, I took a long, hard look at my life. As you're probably aware, within six months of his death, I retired."

"Yes," I murmured. That information was included in the report Decker gave me.

"I like you, Lynx. In fact, I told Emme I thought you were a decent-enough guy."

"What was her response?"

He smiled. "She likened you to a used-car salesman."

"Not surprising."

"My daughter is brilliant. She's one of the most intelligent people I've ever known, and in my line of work, I dealt with geniuses every day."

"I would concur."

"She's also a bit of an eccentric."

Interesting word choice. I preferred it over Irish's quirky.

"I know the two of you share a past, and that's only part of the reason I wanted to talk to you."

I could write tomes filled with accounts of different situations and predicaments I'd found myself in. However, this would rank among the most awkward.

"She cares about you."

"And I, her," I admitted.

Rick stopped walking and turned to face me. "I'm going to ask you straight out to assign someone else to her detail."

Rather than looking at him, I turned toward the water. "Would you be able to do the same if it were Rebecca?"

"I love my wife, Lynx. I also love my daughter. I don't want to see her hurt. I know I can't prevent it from happening, but I can step in and ask you not to make it worse."

"Decker Ashford put a tail on Warrick yesterday. Irish spent the day at MIT."

"I see."

"Until I figure out why, I'm not willing to do what you're asking."

"Fair enough."

Rick continued walking down the beach, and I returned to the house. When I got there, Emerson was in the kitchen.

"There's something I need to ask you."

"Okay."

"What is your personal relationship with Paxon Warrick?"

Her cheeks flushed; there was something she didn't want me to know.

"Emerson?"

She cleared her throat. "After you and my father returned from D.C., I was really angry at both of you. I called Paxon and told him I wanted to return to work. He told me I couldn't."

I nodded. "Did he say why not?"

"He said there was something more in the brush pass. A warning. When I asked him what it was, he told me to talk to you or my father."

That wasn't a reason for Irish to say she shouldn't return. There had to be another reason he didn't want her there.

"Anything else?"

Rather than at me, Emerson looked out the window.

"The day I asked Mario to bring me here, when I was leaving, Paxon asked if he could accompany me downstairs."

"Go on."

"While we were in the elevator, he told me that he'd planned to ask me out."

"He shared that with me."

"That wasn't all. He told me that when you broke my heart, he'd pick up the pieces."

I was processing the information she'd shared when I realized Emerson was staring at me.

"It's okay, Lynx," she said when my eyes met hers. "We both know that once you find Tommy, everything will change."

"You said you weren't seeing each other."

Emerson shook her head. "That isn't what I meant, Lynx."

24

Emerson

"What did you mean?"

"It isn't about Tommy, it's about you and me. We both know that you'll leave and I'll…stay. There's an end date, Lynx. Just like summer, this thing between us will end too."

Lynx grabbed my hand and pulled me into him. "I can't do this anymore."

"Do what?"

"Pretend I don't want to spend every minute kissing the fuck out of you."

His mouth crashed into mine as he backed me against the kitchen island. He lifted me up and set me on the counter, pulled me forward so I was balancing on the edge, and then pushed my legs apart—all the while kissing me so hard I could barely breathe.

I wrapped my arms around him and then slid them down, gripping his ass and pulling him closer so his hot, hard cock rubbed against my wetness.

He gripped the side of my face. "Tell me, Emerson, has it ever been as good with anyone else?"

"Lynx…"

"Tell me," he demanded.

"Never."

"Then why are you so anxious to give it up?"

Before I could answer, he thrust his tongue into my mouth while we ground our bodies against each other.

I was so lost in him that I couldn't figure out what that sound was, until my father stopped clearing his throat and coughed.

I pulled away and buried my face in Lynx's chest.

"Sorry to interrupt, you two. I just wanted you to know that we have tickets to a play in the city tonight. Your mom and I are going to head out now."

"Rick, did you tell them we aren't coming back tonight?" I heard my mother holler from upstairs.

"Not yet, sweetheart."

"Okay, well, we won't be, and since we have plans with Buster and Annie two days later, I don't think we'll return until the end of the week."

Lynx stepped away but not far enough that I could jump down from the counter.

"Have a good time," I murmured, half-hiding my heated face.

"You too," my mom said with a wave as she walked from the staircase straight outside. "We'll lock the door on our way out."

When I heard the car leave, I faced him.

"I want you naked, Emerson."

He settled between my legs, but I couldn't get close enough. I wanted every inch of my body touching his—skin on skin.

"Hold on," he said, putting his hands under my ass.

"What are you doing?"

"Taking you…somewhere. I don't know where."

More than anything, I wanted him to carry me out to the daybed on the back porch. But it was the middle of the day, there were people on the beach, probably the same families who'd heard me screaming at Paxon over the phone a few days ago.

"Put me down."

"I don't want to."

"If you do, I'll take you someplace I think you might like."

"If you're there, I'll like it." He slid me down his body, so I could feel every hard edge of it against my softness.

I took his hand and led him out to the pool, closed the gate behind us, and walked over to the pool house. It was really more like an oversized cabana with two separate sides. One side had a changing room, a small kitchen, even a television, and big, fluffy, terry-cloth-covered chairs to sit in. But the opposite side was where I was taking Lynx.

I flung the double door open and waved my hand for him to come inside.

"Clothes off, Emerson."

Once I was naked, he pushed me down on the bed, spread my legs, and then spread the lips of my pussy.

"Lynx…please…"

"Tell me what you need, Emerson."

I grabbed one of his hands and pushed it between my legs. When he thrust two fingers inside me and his tongue pressed against my clit, my entire body arched as an orgasm seized through me.

I quivered in his arms. "Please," I begged again. My pussy clenched with the need for him to fill me with his cock. When Lynx was inside me, it was as though I felt whole, complete, that our bodies were made to be the perfect fit. "I need you," I begged, urging him up my body.

25

Lynx

As she came apart in my arms, every ounce of possessiveness in me roared to life. I wanted this woman to be mine and only mine. I wanted to spend hours with my head between her tits, sucking, kneading, licking, loving, but I needed something more. I needed her mouth, and when I got it, I didn't want to let it go.

I moved up her body and made love to her mouth with mine like I had her pussy. Her scent, her taste lingered, and I wanted her to know how much I fucking loved it.

Emerson's body writhed beneath mine as I thrust my tongue in her mouth like I planned to thrust my rock-hard cock into her pussy.

I pulled away. If I didn't, I'd spend the next hour just kissing her, and Emerson wanted more. "Spread your legs," I demanded, and she shuddered. Damn, I loved that.

I lined my cock up at her entrance; her eyes were wide as I eased into her. When I was buried as far as I could go, something in me broke loose. Letting myself off the leash, I pounded into her, my pubic bone crashing into her clit with every thrust. I ground myself deeper until I felt her pussy clench on me like a vice.

I moved her hair from her face. "Look at me," I demanded. "Keep your eyes open and look at me."

She did, and a scream broke from her lips. "Lynx, Lynx…" It was a mantra, a cry, all the while, her pussy maintained its strangle-hold on my cock.

When her trembling eased, I pulled away and flipped her over. Emerson groaned. "On all fours." Now that I knew my demands made her crazy with need, I wouldn't stop. When I drove my cock back inside her, she cried out.

"Tell me how good you feel, Emerson."

"I'm going to come again, Lynx."

"Wait," I said, slowing and pulling almost all the way out. I wrapped my arm around her middle and surged into her, driving punctuated thrusts into her drenched pussy. I pounded harder and harder, driving in so deep I was afraid I might hurt her, but when she picked up the pace I'd slowed, I let myself go.

"Emerson," I growled as the most powerful orgasm I'd ever had continued to pulse from within me.

I pulled out and flipped her over, hating how cold and alone I felt when I did. I needed Emerson—to be with her, inside her, to never let her go.

What I felt was so profound, so amazing, I felt myself ready to lay it all out at her feet. "Did I hurt you?" I asked, pushing away feelings that could only be described as inappropriate.

Emerson had a faraway look in her eyes. "Only in the best way."

"What are you thinking?"

She sighed. "I live in Boston. You live…somewhere else…I don't know where you live."

"I live in London." There was no sense attempting to skirt the issue. We had two very different lives, led in two very different places, but I didn't want to dwell on it. Not when the woman I'd fantasized about for three years was naked in my arms.

She pulled away, sat up, and put her legs over the side of the bed.

"Where you going?"

She walked out of the cabana and over to the edge of the pool. Before diving in, she looked over her shoulder. "Swimming," she said with a luscious smile on her face.

26

Emerson

I dove deep, willing the saltwater to wash away the tears that filled my eyes when I thought about Lynx leaving.

I'd known he would. There was never any question that he would return to England or wherever his job took him next.

We spent one night together years ago, and now we'd spent one week. I told myself we'd gotten to know each other, but that was silly. We hadn't scratched the surface. I swam to the other end of the pool, came up for air, and then swam the length back.

As I swam, I felt the ache of my need for physical activity. My body needed to move; I needed to sweat. Even when I worked fourteen- or fifteen-hour days, I found time to run.

When I reached the other end and came up for air again, Lynx was sitting on the edge, his legs dangling in the water.

"Coming in?"

"Watching your naked body glide through the water is mesmerizing."

"Yeah?" I said, pushing my feet from the wall so I floated on my back.

"Holy Mother of God," I heard him mutter. It made me think of something else I didn't know about him.

"Lynx, are you religious?"

He jumped in, swam over to me, and parted my legs; he was tall enough to stand in the water between them. I had wrapped them around his body and paddled with my arms to stay afloat. Instead, he put his arms around my waist and pulled me upright so my breasts were against his chest. I could feel his hardness poking me.

"To answer your question, not in a traditional sense." He angled his head and kissed me. "Right now, it's only at your altar I want to worship." He kissed the tip of my nose. "What about you?"

"No." I don't know why I brought it up. I wanted to ask him everything I didn't know, but not in such a serious way. "Any broken bones?"

"Collarbone. You?"

"Tibial plateau."

"How did you do that?"

"Skiing. What's your favorite color?"

"I've two. Tawny port and ocean blue."

I scrunched my eyes. "That's so specific."

"Yes, it is."

I leaned back and floated with my legs still around Lynx's waist. The light reflected in the water in such a way that I couldn't see his face, but I let my eyes wander down his torso. "How do you stay in such good shape?"

He reached out and tweaked one of my nipples. "I haven't been this week. My regular workouts have fallen by the wayside, I regret to admit."

"I was thinking the same thing earlier."

The next morning when I got out of bed after spending most of the night having orgasm after orgasm rung out of me, I regretted my suggestion that we go for a run on the beach. I regretted stopping at the local gym afterwards even more.

By the time Lynx went through what he referred to as a light workout, I was ready for a massage and a glass of wine followed by twenty-four hours of sleep.

I got the massage and the wine, but sleep? Not so much.

—:—

My parents ended up staying in the city until Friday, and then my mother called to ask if I wanted them to stay longer.

"This is your house," I said when she asked if I was absolutely sure it was okay for them to return to the Cape.

"We wanted to give you and Lynx some privacy."

"Mom, please."

"I might've been able to talk your father into staying away, but I think there's something he wants to discuss with Lynx. After our dinner with Buster and Annie, the two have been talking more frequently. Oh, wait. What did you say, Rick?" It sounded like my mom put her hand over the phone. "Honey, your dad wants to talk with you. Hold on."

"Emme?"

"Hi, Dad."

"Listen, there's been a slight change of circumstance since your mom's been on the phone with you. I'm going to need you and Lynx to come into the city."

"Is everything okay?"

"I hope so." Dad cleared his throat. "We'll talk about it when you get here."

After I'd hung up and gone to look for Lynx, I could tell he'd just ended a conversation similar to mine.

"My dad wants us to come into the city."

Lynx eyes were hooded. "Yes."

"What's going on?"

"I'm not exactly certain."

It looked more like he did know, but didn't want to tell me.

"Lynx?"

"I've arranged for helicopter transport. It will arrive in approximately twenty minutes."

"I'll get my things together."

When the helicopter landed in the same place it had before, Lynx took my bags and pulled me toward it even though the blades hadn't stopped turning. "Keep your head down," he shouted.

He climbed in and then held his hand out for me to do the same.

"Emerson, this is Angel." He motioned to the woman sitting in the pilot's seat. I put on the headset she handed me.

"Nice to meet you, Emerson," she said. "I've heard a lot about you."

"Nice to meet you too," I said, turning in my seat to glare at Lynx.

"What?" he mouthed, holding up both of his hands.

I wouldn't say anything now when she could hear me, but Angel wasn't just pretty, she was fucking gorgeous. Model gorgeous. Like Tommy, she was so ridiculously beautiful, they could be featured in an underwear ad together.

When we landed, Mario was waiting to transport us by car to my building.

Once we were on our way, I folded my arms and looked out the side window.

"What's bothering you?" Lynx asked.

"Why did you talk to her about me?"

"It isn't what you think."

"If it isn't what I think, what is it?"

"It wasn't me. It was Saint."

"Is she his girlfriend?"

He looked confused. "Angel?"

I nodded.

"No."

"Is she your girlfriend?"

"That isn't worthy of a response."

"What did Tommy tell her about me?"

He shook his head. "It isn't important."

"It is to me."

We were in front of my building, and Lynx hadn't said anything more.

"Tell me," I repeated.

"Emerson…"

"I need to know."

"Very well. He told her that one day he'd marry you."

27

Lynx

"That's not logical."

No, it wasn't. Nor did it make sense that Saint had told me they'd been seeing each other prior to his disappearance. But my concern now had little to do with my missing agent, at least on the surface.

I pressed the button for the lift, mulling over the proposal Decker Ashford had outlined in our earlier phone call, as I had been since I rang off. It didn't make sense either, and that Emerson's father was willing to go along with it, was even more worrisome.

I walked Emerson to her door and saw that the keypad I'd requested had been installed.

"Oh! What's this? I mean, I know what it is, but what do I do? Well, I know what to do, but is there a code? Has someone programmed my handprint in? How did they get my—"

"I know your code."

"You do?"

"Yes."

"Oh." She tapped her finger on her bottom lip. "Why?"

"Because it's my birthday, followed by my initials."

"When's your birthday?"

"Twenty-three December."

"And your initials?"

"LCE."

"Lennox…"

"Charles Edgemon."

Emerson cocked her head to the side and smiled. "How cute is that?" She punched in the code, rested her hand on the pad, and the door opened.

If only I weren't so angry at Decker and her father, I might have smiled too, but right now, I couldn't muster more than a scowl.

With a shoulder shrug, Emerson took her bags to the bedroom and then rejoined me in the apartment's main room.

"What now?" she asked.

"Your father and Decker should be here momentarily." I hadn't asked specifically, but I assumed the apartment had been swept for spyware of any kind.

Emerson walked over to the window and looked out. Her arms were folded, and she was tapping her lower lip with her fingertip again. She took a deep breath and then turned toward me. "Something is bothering you, and it has nothing to do with Tommy or Dr. Benjamin."

I nodded.

"It's something to do with me, isn't it?"

"It's best we wait—"

"No, Lynx. If it involves me, I want to know what it is."

"Very well. Decker has had Irish under surveillance for several days. He has spent the majority of the last few at MIT."

"I see."

"I'm unaware of how, but yesterday, Decker arranged for Irish to gain access to your office."

Her eyes opened wide.

"Decker planted information which he has reason to believe Irish discovered." I scrubbed my face with my hand. "There is a second part to this that involves you."

Before I could go on, there was a knock at the door. I answered it before Emerson could, wishing I had time to speak to the two gentlemen who joined us, alone.

"Emme," Rick Charles said, taking his daughter in his arms. I thought about the last conversation he and

I had and his warning not to hurt his daughter. Wasn't what he and Decker were suggesting the antithesis of his warning to me?

"Let's sit," I suggested.

"I'll stand," Emerson replied, motioning for the three of us to sit. Only Decker and her father did.

I turned to Decker. "I've made Emerson aware of the events taking place through yesterday."

He nodded and looked up at her. "We have reason to believe that Paxon Warrick has been gathering intelligence that he is selling to the Chinese."

By the time he finished his sentence, I was by Emerson's side. I led her to the sofa and sat next to her.

"He's a double agent?" she asked.

"We believe so," Decker answered.

"Lynx said this involves me somehow."

"We need to be certain," said her father, leaning forward in his chair. "In order for that to happen, we need you to return to your office."

"To feed him specific information?"

"That's right," Rick answered, looking from her to me. "Emme, you should know that Lynx is not in favor of this."

"Why not?" she asked me directly.

"In order for this to work, the two of you will need to be alone."

"We worked alone for weeks."

Simultaneously, Decker's and my mobile went off.

"Excuse me," he said, standing and leaving Emerson's apartment.

"What's going on?" she asked when I stood as well.

"There's a press conference taking place."

Both Emerson and her father followed me to Saint's apartment. Once inside, I saw Decker had donned a headset. When I approached the monitors he was studying, I could see that the news ticker on the bottom of the screen read, *Breaking News/Special Report*. The headline at the top of the screen read, "Two Americans and two Brits arrested in China, sentenced to death on drug-trafficking charges." There on the dais to the side of the podium where a Chinese official stood, were Dr. Adam Benjamin and Niven St. Thomas. Next to them, stood two other men.

I was about to call Z when my mobile rang with his call.

"Have you seen?" he asked.

"Just now."

"The execution is scheduled in two days' time."

"Has the team mobilized?"

"Affirmative. How soon can you and Ashford do the same?" Z asked.

I made my way to the back of the apartment, walked into Saint's office, and closed the door behind me. "I'll be on the next transport out, but Ashford will not be with me." I went on to explain what we believed about Irish Warrick. "He needs to stay to see this through."

"Understood," said Z. "Angel as well?"

"Yes. She's going into MIT undercover."

There was a knock at the door, and I opened it. Decker stepped inside. When he motioned, I put the mobile on speaker.

"Decker is here," I told Z.

"Fill us in."

Decker cleared his throat. "The U.S. Ambassador has made arrangements to transport Lynx to Beijing. He'll be accompanying him under the auspice of further negotiation. They'll meet with the U.K. Ambassador to China, and both will insist on an audience with the prisoners to confirm their health and well-being before making the deal to deliver the dissidents. The team will be ready to move in upon Lynx's signal. His job will be to get the two ambassadors out before the Chinese discover the extraction. Questions?"

"Lynx?" asked Z.

"None."

Decker looked at his mobile and then up at me. "Transport will be here in fifteen."

Which left me exactly that long to say goodbye to Emerson.

28

Emerson

"Lynx is waiting for you in the office," said Decker.

The time for him to leave had arrived, and as much as my brain understood and accepted that fact, my heart ached. Our magical summer was coming to an end far too soon, but I couldn't ask him not to go. Tommy's and Dr. Benjamin's lives were at stake.

"Hi," I said, standing in the doorway.

"I don't have much time."

When he held out his hand, I took it and let him pull me into an embrace. "Be safe," I whispered.

Lynx cupped my cheek with his palm and stared into my eyes. "I wish I could say I'll be back, but I can't."

"I understand."

"Decker will be with you tomorrow, as will Angel."

"Angel? Why?"

"She'll be undercover."

I didn't like it, but it wasn't something I would argue with Lynx about now.

"I wish we had more time."

"I do too."

"Emerson, I—"

I put my fingertips on his lips. Whatever he'd say now would be forced, and I didn't want to hear it in his voice. In the course of the last several days, there was a reason we hadn't discussed anything beyond this mission. Reality had been lurking in the background of every conversation we had. It had risen to the surface on a number of occasions when one or both of us were willing to say out loud what we were both thinking.

Once Saint and Dr. Benjamin were safe, they, along with Lynx, would return to the U.K. End of story; it didn't include a happily ever after.

I brought my lips to his and kissed him. He held me so tight that it made me wonder if he was having as hard a time letting go as I was.

He pulled away and brushed my hair from my face. He rested his hand near the place where I'd cut my head. "You need to get the staples removed."

"Yes."

"Contact Stephen."

"I don't want to inconvenience him."

"Contact Stephen," he repeated, kissing my forehead. "He'll take care of you."

"Okay," I murmured. The truth was, I couldn't imagine going to anyone else—inconvenient or not.

"There are things I want to say…"

"Lynx, please don't."

He nodded and kissed me again. It was the kind of kiss he'd given me when we had sex. It was deep and hard and packed full of the emotion neither of us would allow ourselves to admit we were feeling.

"Goodbye, Emerson."

"Goodbye, Lynx."

I walked with him to the elevator, where he kissed me once more. When the door opened and he stepped inside, I couldn't look at him. I turned before the door closed and walked to my apartment.

I felt like a boulder of sadness was resting on my chest, but it didn't hurt nearly as bad as my heart ached. Why? God, I'd known this was coming. I'd reminded myself of it often enough over the course of the last three weeks. Three weeks? It felt like months. It was said that doing something twenty-one days in a row made it a habit. It hadn't taken that long for Lynx to become a habit I wanted to continue doing for the rest of my life.

I rested my forehead against the door while I punched in the code, *2312LCE,* and then pressed my palm on the pad.

The door opened, and when I walked inside, my mom was sitting on the sofa, waiting for me.

"Lynx is gone," I told her, and she nodded.

"Come here," she said, holding her hand out to me.

I sat beside her, she put her arm around me, and I rested my head on her shoulder. "I knew this was coming."

"It doesn't make it any easier, sweetheart."

I wiped the tears that slid down my cheeks away, wishing I could stop them from falling.

"It's okay to be sad, you know."

"It's silly."

"No, Emme, it's normal. You know what we should do?"

I shook my head.

"Eat."

"You don't want to cook in my kitchen, Mom."

"You're right. We'll get your father to take us out for dinner," said my mom.

"I'm not that hungry."

"You will be when you see where he's taking us."

I shook my head. I could guarantee my father had no idea where my mother would be insisting they go.

"This place is such a tourist trap," I said when my father drove up to the only place in Boston that made lobster the way my mother liked.

"Everyone says that, but I bet ninety percent of the people having dinner here tonight are from Boston."

"Sorry about this," I said to Decker, who my mother had insisted join us regardless of his protests. "But unless you want hundred-dollar lobster, they don't have much else."

"Lobster's good. Can't find it much back home."

"Where is home?"

"I live on a ranch just north of Austin, Texas. You want a steak? Come visit."

I smiled. "Thanks, Decker."

"You're welcome," he said, as though he understood that him being along gave me the moral support I needed to get through not just tonight, but the next few days too.

The maître d' led us to the back of the restaurant to a private dining room.

"We have business to discuss," my father murmured, escorting me into the room.

Once we'd ordered dinner and our drinks were delivered, my parents stood. My father walked my mother to the door and closed it behind her after she'd walked out.

"Decker, do you want to fill Emme in on what you've uncovered?"

"As you know, U.S. intelligence—the CIA specifically—has suffered major setbacks in China."

I was aware that the agency's once-robust espionage network had been falling apart for the last five years. In that time, dozens of CIA informants in China had disappeared, either jailed or killed.

"The agency has been convinced there was a mole feeding information to Chinese intelligence officers."

"And you suspect Paxon?"

"More than suspect, Emme," said my father.

"While it wasn't his original mission, Saint was also investigating Irish based on information he was given by Dr. Benjamin."

"Dr. Benjamin?" I tapped my lip with my fingertip. "You think he left proof. That's why Paxon has been at MIT even though I haven't. It's also why he didn't want me to return last week."

"There's more," said my father, covering my hand with his.

"What?" I asked, looking between him and Decker.

"There's evidence suggesting that Irish may have had a hand in Saint's and Benjamin's disappearances."

"What do you need me to do?"

"Two things," said Decker. "First, find the evidence Dr. Benjamin left, and then lead Paxon to the remaining evidence we planted."

"Wait. You don't have Benjamin's evidence already?"

Decker shook his head. "I have enough on Irish without it, but finding it would give us the names of the people Irish has been working with."

"You don't think Irish knows where it is?" I asked.

"Even if he did, it's unlikely he'd know what he was looking at," said my dad.

"It's in code. That's where you come in," I said to him.

He and Decker both nodded.

The door opened, and my mother walked back in, followed by two waiters carrying our lobster, signaling the end of our conversation.

My parents went home after dropping Decker and me at my building.

"You up for doing this tonight?" he asked when the elevator opened to my floor.

"I don't have any choice."

Decker went over everything that had been planted in my office, as well as what he believed I should be looking for when I got there tomorrow.

Something occurred to me. "Wait a minute."

Decker raised his head.

"We need to get my father back over here."

"Why?"

"Because I have what we're looking for."

Three hours later, my father raised his head and smiled. "I found it."

As much as I wanted to be there when Paxon was arrested, I knew I shouldn't be. It would only complicate what would already be a tenuous situation. My father didn't go either. Instead, he, my mother, and I went out for breakfast.

We were just finishing our coffee when my mother reached over and touched my hand and then motioned to the television above the bar.

"CIA Officer Arrested for Conspiracy to Spy for China," the headline read. I watched as Paxon Warrick was led away in handcuffs. Off to the side, I could see the top of Decker's head. These weren't men that needed the glory that came along with a press conference. No, men like Decker, Lynx, and even my father, were the kind of people who worked behind the scenes, keeping the rest of us safe from the atrocities that took place daily around the world.

"I want to leave MIT," I blurted. I couldn't say it was something I'd thought about. I just decided, and once I had, I knew I couldn't go back.

29

Lynx

"I wanted you to know Irish Warrick was arrested a little over an hour ago," said Decker when he called shortly after our plane landed in London.

He explained that Emerson had Dr. Benjamin's reports with her all along.

"Those bloody bags full of bricks," I mumbled. I should've known.

"It didn't take her father long before he pieced the code together. Once he had, there was no reason for us to execute the rest of the plan."

I was relieved there hadn't been any need for Emerson to interact with Irish or put herself in unnecessary danger.

"I sent you the full report."

"Thanks, Decker."

"Godspeed, Lynx. To the crew also."

"I'll pass it on."

I intentionally hung up before asking where Emerson was now. That was no longer any of my business, but, God, did I miss her. When I closed my eyes, I saw her face and smelled her skin. I could even feel her touch and her soft lips, her tongue, everything. Besides my parents, I'd never missed anyone. Not even Keon. But Emerson, I didn't just miss her, I longed for her with a yearning like none other I'd ever experienced. I'd walked away from her this morning without a word about when I might see her again. It's what we both accepted to be our reality, but that didn't change the fact I'd give anything to have the fantasies I had about what our life would be like together become our new reality.

I sighed and opened Deck's report and read it while I waited for our next flight.

Paxon "Irish" Warrick, it appeared, had been passing classified intelligence reports to the Chinese dating back as early as seven years ago. For betraying his country and being directly responsible for the loss of life of several of his fellow agents, Irish pocketed a little over five million dollars.

There was no clear understanding of why he did it, except for the money.

I'd just ordered a pint in the private lounge where the ambassador and I were waiting when my mobile rang again.

"Hello, Cope," I said.

"You've been expecting my call."

"I have."

"Listen, Lynx, I'm sorry I couldn't read you in on the investigation into Irish, but it was vital that he be left in place long enough that he'd eventually show his hand. We had to stop the bloodbath, and in order to do so, we needed to know who he was working with."

"Understood," I said, and I meant it. There was no reason for him to read me in last week. The investigation details were need-to-know only. It would've worked exactly the same way if the situation were MI6 led rather than CIA.

I got the signal from the ambassador's detail that we were about to board the plane. In a matter of hours, one of two things would happen. Either I'd be on my way back to London with Saint and Dr. Benjamin, or one or more of us would be dead. That was how missions like this worked. I knew my brother, Rile, and Grinder were feeling the same way I was.

"I need to ring off, Cope."

"Godspeed, Lynx. Bring 'em home."

—:—

I spent the first part of the ten-hour flight from London to Beijing briefing my second in command for this mission, Damon "Typhon" Morgan. The code name given to the MI6 agent was after one of the deadliest creatures in Greek mythology.

While the official position of MI6 was that agents were not permitted to break any laws outside of the U.K. that would be illegal within, or in other words, agents and officers did not possess a "license to kill," there wasn't a single one of us who didn't know that was as far from the truth as our jobs got.

It wasn't something any of us were proud of, even Typhon. Taking a human life was always considered last resort, but if it came to that, no one I'd ever known was as deadly as the man sitting in front of me. I had access to Typhon's kill record, and he'd exceeded mine in his first two years of duty.

His presence, along with two CIA operatives, was necessitated by the two people we were personally tasked with keeping alive throughout the course of the mission—both the U.S. and the U.K. Ambassadors to China.

Once Typhon and I were finished reviewing the plan, he went to brief the two CIA agents while I met with the U.K. Ambassador, briefing her on what would be required of her in the extraction's aftermath.

There was no question in my mind that the Chinese would want to immediately retaliate, but with two such high profile diplomats, it would be impossible to do so.

One aspect of my job was to ensure the media, part of the entourage also on this flight, was in place at the same time the extraction was taking place. Buster, the more powerful of the two ambassadors in terms of influence as well as personality, knew to immediately ask for a press conference at the same time the Invincible crew brought Dr. Benjamin front and center.

Behind the scenes, the rest of the team would be transporting Saint and the two CIA-operative hostages out of the country.

The meeting had been scheduled to take place at the Great Hall of the People, a state building located at the western edge of Tienanmen Square in Beijing.

It was understood that the prisoners would be brought there in advance, per Ambassador Steven's request. What the Chinese were told was that the seven dissidents who had been extradited in exchange for our men, were being held at the U.S. Embassy. The exchange would take place only after the ambassadors were able to confirm our people were all still alive.

Once the ambassadors and Chinese government officials had completed their introductions, I sent the signal to the Invincible team to proceed. I was escorting the press into the Great Halls' meeting room when I heard gunfire erupt through my earpiece.

"Go, go, go!" I recognized Rile's voice shouting.

"They're in here!" another voice shouted that sounded like my brother's. I made eye contact with Typhon to confirm he was hearing the same thing I was.

"Got 'em," shouted Rile, followed a few seconds later by, *"We're out."*

That was my cue to meet whomever from the team was escorting Dr. Benjamin into the hall. I stepped out and made eye contact with first the doctor, and then Grinder. I knew immediately that whatever he was about to tell me, was news I didn't want to receive.

30

Emerson

We left the city the next day and went down the Cape. My parents seemed to realize that I had too much on my mind to talk, and left me on my own for the most part.

I took walks on the beach at sunrise, slept on the back-porch daybed, and swam. I spent too much time in the pool cabana, lying on the bed where Lynx and I had last had sex, imagining he was beside me.

That's where I was when I heard my mother shouting my name. I ran into the house, blood pumping through my veins so hard it was all I could hear.

"Look," she said, pointing to the television and grasping my father's hand. There on the screen stood the man I'd grown up calling Uncle Buster—now the U.S. Ambassador to China. On the other side of him stood the woman I recognized as his British counterpart. To her right, stood Dr. Adam Benjamin.

I listened as they thanked the Chinese government for their cooperation in freeing the doctor, mistakenly arrested for a crime he didn't commit. There was no mention of the other men who had been arrested.

My mother reached out her hand to me, and I sat beside her on the sofa.

"Where do you suppose Lynx is," she whispered.

Before I could speculate, my father's cell phone rang. He stood and walked out to the back porch before answering the call.

When he came back inside, his face was ashen.

"What is it?" I asked.

"Keon, Lynx's brother, was shot during the extraction. He's alive, but his condition is unknown."

31

Lynx

Three Months Later

I left Z's office, no closer to making a decision than when I arrived. He'd asked when I planned to return to active duty; it was a question I was unable to answer.

I'd spent the last three months by my brother's side, at first in a hospital in Seoul, and then in London.

While the bullet that hit him during Saint and Dr. Benjamin's extraction hadn't been life-threatening, it had been damaging. He'd undergone three surgeries and was just now getting full mobility back in his right arm.

It was his mental state that worried me the most. There were many days when my brother's depression was so great that I refused to leave him alone, even to sleep.

I'd given up my residency suite at the hotel, since it was too small for both of us to stay there, and rented a flat near the hospital so when he was able to leave, he had a comfortable place to stay.

My brother's spirits improved in direct correlation to the movement he regained in his arm. As much as I was against it, he was insisting on returning to Texas as soon as possible, and I planned to travel with him.

"Did you tell him?" asked Saint when I pulled up a seat next to him in the pub.

I shook my head. "I haven't made my final decision yet."

"Yes, you have, you liar."

Saint was right. Keon had been visited by all of the Invincibles' partners at least once during his hospital stay, but Decker had come more than the other two.

During his last visit, he'd approached me with an offer to join up with their firm. Initially, my answer had been a resounding no. However, after I realized my brother was in on it, I agreed to reconsider.

Keon asking wasn't my only reason, as I'm sure they knew. If I were to partner with them, it would also allow me to spend a great deal more time in the States.

"You'll never believe who I saw the other day," Saint said, motioning to the barmaid to pour me a pint.

"Who?"

"Angel."

"How is she?"

Saint shook his head. "Same as always. Smarter, funnier, prettier than me, and still able to drink me under the table."

I laughed. "She is all those things. Deadlier too."

"She and I got to talking about a certain helicopter ride the two of you shared."

"Yeah?"

"She told me she still regretted telling you what I confessed to her on one of those nights I crashed beneath a pub table."

I took a long, slow drink, silently warning my friend that this was not a conversation he wanted to start.

"Look, you have to admit, the woman is beguiling."

"Tread carefully, Saint. In fact, a change in subject would be your smartest tack."

He shook his head and looked down at the bar. "I meant it. At the time anyway."

I slammed my now-empty pint on the bar. "Do you have a bloody death wish?"

Saint motioned to the barmaid, who poured each of us another. "Bring us two shots of Irish too, would you?"

When she delivered the shots, Saint looked into my eyes. "Go see her, Lynx."

I downed the whiskey and emptied my pint before I responded. "We both knew what it was, and that was temporary."

"I have reason to believe you might be wrong, at least on Charlie's—err, Emerson's—part."

I grabbed Saint by the neck and slammed him up against the wall. "This is not a game," I seethed. "You dare to speak to me of the woman I…"

He held up both hands.

When I let go, he straightened his jacket and sat down as if nothing had happened, not even a single hair was out of place on the bastard's head.

"What, Lynx? The woman you, what?"

I watched as he signaled the barmaid again, on the verge of slamming him up against the wall a second time.

"Start talking, Saint, while you're still able."

—:—

Snow? Truly? It was the beginning of December, and not just snow, a blizzard. It was a miracle Mario had been able to get to the airport at all. The ride from there to the apartment building had been harrowing, which reminded me of Emerson and how she'd said she wouldn't ride in any car with the man we'd referred to as Mario Andretti. I smiled at the memory.

I reached over the seat, handed him some cash, and shook his hand. "Thank you for coming out in a snow-storm to get me here."

"Let me know when you need me again, Mr. Edgemon. Always happy to drive you anywhere you need to go."

"Call me Lynx, and I appreciate it." I got out of the car and grabbed my bag. Instead of going straight inside, I stood at the building's entrance, remembering the first day I set foot in it and found the woman I'd been looking for, dreaming about, yet never dreaming I'd actually find. What I'd give to see Emerson's beau-tiful face walking out as I walked in again.

"Mr. Edgemon," I heard a familiar voice say once I stepped inside the lobby. "Welcome back."

"Mr. Bridges," I answered, walking over to shake his hand. "It's nice to see you."

"Saint completed the paperwork you requested. Let me get it for you."

While I waited for him to retrieve the lease transfer and extension, I thought again about whether my hang-ing onto the apartment was folly.

"Here it is," he said, handing me the envelope. "And let me be the first to officially welcome you to the building."

"Thanks," I said, holding up the envelope, "for this too."

He stood in the doorway of his office while I waited for the lift. "Was there anything else, Mr. Bridges?"

"Call me Baxter, and no, not really." He shook his head, went into his office, and closed the door behind him.

I rode the lift to the eighth floor, toying with knocking on Emerson's door before dropping my bag at Saint's—my—apartment. Given it was after nine, it would probably be best to wait until tomorrow.

When the lift's door opened, I heard a man's voice coming from the direction of Emerson's apartment. "I love you, too," he said, closing her door behind him.

"Hi," he said when he saw me staring. "Can I help you with something?"

"Who are you?"

"I'm David," he said, chuckling. "Who are you?"

I heard Emerson's door open and held my breath. Had she really found someone already? Someone who loved her too?

"You forgot your hat," I heard a familiar voice say. "Oh, Lennox, hi," said Rashid, handing the hat to the man I now guessed was his boyfriend. I held the door of the lift open as they kissed goodbye.

"Nice to meet you, Lennox," said David, as he stepped inside.

"Um, Rashid," I said as he walked back to the apartment.

"Yes?"

"Is Emerson at home?"

He cocked his head. "I'm confused."

"Emerson," I pointed at the door. "Her apartment?"

"Emme doesn't live here anymore. David and I sublet the place from her."

32

Emerson

"Professor Charles?"

I raised my head when one of my female students approached the dais at the end of my lecture. "Yes?"

"I just wanted to thank you for the insight you shared today, and also…"

"What is it?"

"I really admire you. Having you here, well, it gives me hope."

The student walked out of the lecture hall before I found my voice to thank her. Little did she know what her words meant to me, today especially.

When I left MIT, I had no desire to work for another university. In fact, I had no desire to do much of anything. I was sitting in my apartment in Boston, feeling quite sorry for myself when the landline I often forgot I had, rang. I thought about letting it go to voicemail, but given I didn't know how to retrieve messages, or even if I'd set up an incoming message, I decided to answer it.

"Emme?" a familiar voice said.

"Uncle Buster? Why are you calling this number?"

"You aren't an easy woman to get a hold of, young lady. In fact, when I tried to leave you a message, I was told your inbox was full."

"I'm sorry."

"How about you meet your uncle for lunch this week?"

I'd agreed, never expecting what would come of it.

Two weeks later, I went to work for the NWC—the U.S. Naval War College, in Newport Rhode Island.

Yes, both my father and Uncle Buster pulled strings to secure my interview, but had assured me once my foot was in the door, the rest was up to me.

Much to my surprise, earlier this morning, after only being here two months, I was offered a National Security Affairs associate professorship in the Strategy and Policy Department.

I didn't pay a lot of attention when I heard the door open and close at the top of the hall. It was probably a student looking for a quiet place to read or arriving early for their next class.

I gathered the papers and books scattered on the table next to the lectern and stuffed them into my bags.

It was my last class of the week, and tomorrow night I had a real treat planned—a celebration dinner with my best friend.

It had been three weeks since I last saw Nora, and I couldn't wait to get caught up. Living in Newport made it easier for her and I to get together; Providence was only forty minutes away. The drive to Boston, where my parents were for the winter, or to Cape Cod were both twice as long. Not that I'd be going down the Cape. If I did, I'd be alone, and I could do that here.

I hadn't exactly made friends since I'd moved to Newport and, in this case, it was for lack of trying. Several of the other professors often invited me to join them for drinks, but I always politely declined.

Since I'd never accepted, I couldn't say for certain what they talked about, but there were a plethora of land-mine topics I knew I wanted to steer clear of.

First was China. It was still my area of expertise, and I didn't mind teaching it, but talking about it outside of a class would lead me down a bunny trail of memories I'd just as soon avoid.

The other topic I could see exploding in my face was any talk of families. Don't get me wrong, I love my parents, but when the other professors started talking about their husbands, wives, or significant others, like

I assumed they would, there'd be no amount of alcohol that could numb the pain I knew I'd feel.

I shoved the last of my class materials into my bags and was getting ready to hoist them on my shoulders when I heard the footsteps of someone headed my way. I raised my hand to block the glare of the lights shining on me, but still couldn't see anyone.

"Why don't you let me help you with those," a deliciously English-accented voice called out to me. I left my bags on the table and ran up the steps.

"Tommy? Is that really you?"

"Yes, Charlie, it's really me," he said, picking me up and twirling me in a circle.

When he set me on my feet, I rested my hands on his arms and looked into his sapphire-blue eyes. They'd always mesmerized me, especially since people always commented on mine. Next to his, though, mine were dull and lackluster.

"You look good," I said, letting my gaze drift from his perfectly coiffed blond hair down to the charcoal gray turtleneck sweater and jeans he wore, all the way to a pair of those driving loafers no one ever wore socks with. Didn't their feet get cold? And what was the point in having particular shoes for driving if you wore them everywhere else?

"Did you hear me?" I heard him ask.

"What? Oh! No, I'm sorry. I was just thinking about your shoes. They aren't really shoes, but that's what I was thinking about."

Tommy gave me one of his high-voltage, ultra-white, teeth-filled, melt-most-women's-panties smiles, and I waited for a weak-kneed swoon. None came.

"So…what are you doing here?"

"As I said only a moment ago, I've come to spend some time with my favorite girl."

I cocked my head and studied him. "How did you find me?"

He walked around me to get my bags. "I'll tell you over a glass of Amarone."

When we exited the main building, Tommy pointed toward the parking lot.

"Oh, I don't usually drive. It's only a mile to my apartment."

"You walk a mile carrying these?" he asked, holding out my bags.

"They aren't that heavy," I said, trying to take one from him.

"They are, and no, you may not carry one. I've hired a car, by the way. It's in the lot."

I followed him to what looked like a brand new Jaguar. "You can hire—I mean, rent—these?"

He put the bags in the trunk and then came around to open my door. "I may have misled you, I've actually borrowed it."

"From whom?"

"A friend. I believe you met her. Angel."

"She drives a nice car." I got in, but Tommy didn't close my door. I felt his finger on my cheek.

"How are you, sweet Charlie?"

I turned my head away to hide my tears, and he closed the door. Before he came around, I took a deep breath, squared my shoulders, and wiped tears.

"Wine makes everything better," he said, starting the car and driving straight to my apartment without asking where it was.

I'd been right earlier. Anyone could easily find me if they wanted to.

"Come, sweetness," he said, opening my door after pulling into my driveway. "Second story, yes?"

I stopped and put my hands on my hips. "How do you know that?"

"I promise we'll discuss everything. Let's get you inside."

I watched Tommy move about the room with his usual grace. He was such a beautiful man, and if I hadn't met Lynx, or met him again, maybe I could fall for him.

"Here's to you," he said, handing me a glass of wine poured from a bottle he'd brought with him. We toasted and I took a sip.

"This is really good. What did you say it was?"

"Amarone della Valpolicella. It's my favorite wine."

I took another sip and sat on the sofa; Tommy came and sat beside me.

"We have some unfinished business between us."

"Tommy, I—"

"Tsk, tsk. It's not polite to interrupt, and I know for a fact that your mother would be appalled by your ill manners." He winked and I smiled.

I folded my arms and turned so I was facing him.

"The kiss," he said, looking into my eyes.

"Yes. The kiss. What was that about, Tommy?"

He scrubbed his face with his hand and sighed. It may have been the first time I saw the man without the shroud of composure enveloping him.

"I've rehearsed what I was going to say so many times, and yet, here I am, speechless."

I put my hand on his arm. "We don't have to talk about it."

"Ah, but we do because you, my beautiful girl, mean the world to me."

"It was just so…unexpected."

He reached his arm across the back of the sofa, touching my shoulder with his fingertips. "You have no idea how lovely you are." He shook his head and smiled. "Or, how bruised my ego was when you were… what is the word…aghast."

"Surprised. Not aghast. Seriously, though, why did you do it?"

"Call it cocky optimism, I suppose. I was certain my affection would be reciprocated. So," he slapped his legs with his hands. "Not the case. My broken heart has since mended, and quite a good thing since I understand your heart belongs to another."

"My heart? No. There's no one else. I mean, there was, sort of, but I'm sure you know that Lynx, we… uh…met a few years ago. Actually, I'm not certain I'd call it meeting since we didn't even know each other's names. Well, I knew his name was Lynx and he knew mine was Emerson, but we didn't know last names. And then, well, I met him at our building…"

Tommy smiled. "It's okay, Charlie. I know everything that happened."

"Everything?"

He shook his head. "No, not everything." He put his hand on his heart. "I couldn't have withstood the pain of hearing details, but, yes, I know about you and Lynx."

"There isn't any 'me and Lynx.'"

"About that, sweetheart, we need to talk."

33

Lynx

I walked into the apartment that was now mine, at least that's what the lease said. It didn't look much different than it had when Saint was the primary resident. The wardrobes were empty, but I'd never checked to see what, if anything, was in them previously.

The refrigerator and cupboards were as bare as they had been when Emerson and I were first here together, which reminded me the chai tea cup might still be here.

I opened another cupboard, and there it was. Someone had obviously washed it but hadn't known it belonged to Rashid's father's store. Perhaps I should walk down the hallway and give it to him. Then he'd have to take it over himself. Instead, I set it on the island so I'd remember to deliver it myself when I left.

And I was leaving. Without Emerson living here, there was no reason for me to do so either.

When Saint assured me he had reason to believe Emerson might be interested in a longer-term relationship with me, he didn't mention that she'd moved out of her apartment. I'm sure it would be easy enough for me to find where she'd gone. But was that fair? Just like the morning I woke in the hotel room to find her gone, I found myself questioning the ethics of using my job or connections to find her.

Since I was in Boston for the weekend with nothing to do, I decided to call Stephen. Maybe he and Nora would be up to me visiting.

My call went to voicemail, so I sent my cousin a text message instead. While I waited for him to ring me back, I decided to take the ceramic cup across the street to Rashid's father's store.

It was brutally cold outside, reminding me of the harrowing ride I experienced from the airport. Perhaps driving to Providence this weekend wouldn't be the best idea after all.

When I ran across Boylston and into the corner market. A man I didn't recognize was behind the counter.

"I believe this belongs to your store," I said, setting it on the counter. No sooner had I done so, than Rashid's father came walking up from the rear of the store. "My apologies for returning this so late," I said, pointing to the cup.

"It belongs to Emme," he said, not bothering to make eye contact.

I had no idea what to do next. Should I take it back to her apartment and ask Rashid to keep it for her? That was probably the only viable option.

I thanked the two men and walked out of the market without purchasing any food. It would be easy enough for me to dine out somewhere tonight. If the weather improved, perhaps I'd catch a flight back to Austin in the morning. I was about to walk into the diner next door when my mobile rang.

"Lennox, it's Stephen. I got your text. What a coincidence that we're both in town at the same time again."

"Thanks for getting back to me, what are you and Nora doing in Boston?"

"It's actually Brian and I. Since we were on our own tonight, we decided to do some early Christmas shopping. Wretched weather for it, though."

I told him about my less-than-pleasant ride from the airport.

"We're about to walk into a restaurant. Would you like to join us?"

"Would love to. Where?"

"It's a place I'm sure you know, the Brazilian restaurant on Park Drive."

"I don't know it, but if it's on Park, I'll be there shortly."

I rang off and hailed the cab that just dropped two people off at the bar next door to the diner.

"Do you know a Brazilian place on Park?" I asked the driver. He nodded, but otherwise didn't answer before we sped off.

Less than five minutes later, he pulled up in front of the small restaurant. I could see that Stephen and Brian were the only two people sitting inside. I got out and thanked the man, giving him a generous tip, given the weather.

The smells wafting from the place I was about to walk into were divine.

Stephen met me halfway to their table, and we embraced. "You've never been here?" he asked as he led me back to where Brian was waiting. "Surprising," he said when I shook my head.

"Why is that?"

He studied me as though I was daft, similar to the way Rashid's father often looked at me. "It's just that Emerson recommended it to us."

"I see," I muttered and opened my menu. "When was this?"

"Earlier today when I called Nora to let her know we'd be spending the evening in town." Stephen put his hand on my shoulder. "You're looking a little piqued. Everything all right?"

I opened and closed my eyes, trying to bring the menu items into focus, and cleared my throat. "I'm fine."

"I have to admit, I'm a bit shocked that Emerson would make plans with Nora tonight given you're in town."

"She doesn't know."

"Ah. I see. Surprising her, then?"

I set the menu on the table since I couldn't focus on making a selection. "That was my plan. However, she no longer resides where she used to."

"That would make a right long commute." The look on Stephen's face changed as though things suddenly became clearer. "She didn't tell you she moved to Newport?"

I rested my elbows on the table and leaned forward. "I haven't spoken to Emerson since I left in September."

My cousin shook his head. "Bloody hell! Are you serious?"

34

Emerson

Just as I got to the bottom of the stairs, a car pulled up; I opened the front passenger door and climbed in.

"You really didn't have to drive all the way down here. I could've met you halfway," I said to Nora, reaching across the console to hug her.

"First of all, it isn't that far, and secondly, the girls got a decent nap on the way."

I looked behind me to where Eleanor and Elizabeth were both asleep in their car seats, secretly wishing they were awake so I could hear their sweet voices as they called out for their Auntie Em.

"Where are you going?" I asked when she pulled out onto the main thoroughfare.

"We're celebrating. It's a surprise."

I don't know what I would've done the last three months if it weren't for my friendship with Nora. She and my mother were the only two people I confided in about Lynx, admitting that I was truly heartbroken that I hadn't heard a word from him after his mission ended. Logically I knew we'd both agreed that our "summer holiday" was just that. Temporary. With an end date. That didn't stop my heart from aching whenever I thought about him.

"You won't believe who I ran into yesterday afternoon."

She looked over at me and raised a brow.

"Tommy, you know, Saint."

Nora's eyes opened wide. "I knew who you meant, but where did you see him?"

"He showed up at the end of my lecture."

She peeked over her shoulder at the girls, who were still sound asleep.

"What did he want?" she whispered anyway.

"To talk to me about Lynx."

Her furrowed brow softened, and she smiled. "And?"

"I don't know if what I'm about to tell you makes me feel better or worse, but supposedly he's here in the States. Evidently, he's thinking of leaving MI6."

Nora's furrowed brow reappeared, and I held up my hand.

"Before you say anything, I have run the gamut of emotions over the course of the last twenty-four hours, and I change my mind about how I feel hourly."

"I don't understand. Why hasn't he been in contact?"

"According to Tommy, he wasn't sure I'd want to see him."

"That's ridiculous. So, where is he now?"

"Tommy said he wasn't certain, but he thought he might be in Texas…where his brother lives."

"How is his brother? Stephen mentioned he'd had several surgeries."

"You know more than I do."

"How's this?" she said, pulling up to the curb in front of what she knew was my favorite restaurant in Newport.

"I love it," I said, clapping my hands. "I've been craving Brazilian food since Stephen asked where they should eat tonight."

"Let's take a picture," Nora said once the girls were settled in high chairs. She handed her phone to the waiter and then stood next to me behind Eleanor and Elizabeth.

"Stephen will love this," she said, looking through the photos the waiter had taken. "Do you mind if I text it to him?"

"Of course not. Why would I?"

"You know, cell phones at the dinner table."

I laughed. "You have children to set a good example for. You won't offend me."

We were still looking at the menu when her phone vibrated.

"Go ahead."

She smiled. "If you're sure you don't mind."

I rolled my eyes.

"Oh!"

I looked up and watched as she hit the button to lock her phone and stuck it in her purse.

"I thought he was at dinner with Brian."

"He is," she said, not looking up at me.

"Nora?"

"I'm sorry, Emerson. I don't know what to do."

I tapped my lower lip with my finger. "If Stephen sent you a risqué photo, I hope you don't think you're being rude by not showing it to me. On the contrary—"

"That isn't what he sent," she said, slowly taking her phone back out.

Nausea overcame me when she unlocked the screen. "Wait," I said, holding up my hand. "Tell me what it is first."

"Lynx."

I closed my eyes when she handed me the phone, and then slowly opened one. There, between Stephen and Brian, was the man who owned my heart, whether he wanted it or not. I opened my other eye and studied his face. He was smiling, but didn't look happy.

"He's in Boston," I murmured and then looked up at Nora. "Why?"

She shrugged. "Do you want me to ask?"

"No…wait, yes…no. Definitely no. Or…"

"I'll ask later, when we're home."

"Good idea." I tried to focus on the menu, but everything was a blur. I wasn't sure I was even hungry. But this was a celebration dinner, so it would be very rude of me not to order anything. Plus, Nora had driven all the way to Newport, and she brought the girls, so I couldn't ruin dinner just because the man who broke my heart was in Boston and hadn't even tried to get in touch with me. I jumped up when my eyes filled with tears. "Be right back," I said, handing her phone back and racing toward the ladies' room.

When I came back out, I could tell by the look on her face that Nora had responded to Stephen's text.

"What?"

"He planned to surprise you, but 'you don't live in the building anymore.' That's a direct quote."

"How could he not know? Saint knew exactly where to find me."

"You'll have to ask him."

I heard her phone vibrate again.

"Stephen wants to know if it's okay for him to tell him where you are."

I stared into my friend's eyes. Why wouldn't I want him to know? "Is there a reason I shouldn't?" There must be since Tommy didn't tell him. Why didn't Tommy tell him? Nora was typing something on her phone. "What did you say?"

"I gave him the address of the restaurant."

"But Boston is ninety minutes from here."

She typed something else. "Now he has your address. Or Stephen does."

35

Lynx

I studied the photo that Stephen had forwarded to me. Emerson was smiling, but she didn't look happy. It was like the light inside of her had gone out, and I now knew that was my fault.

"You have to be certain, Lennox."

I looked up at my cousin. It was the second time he gave me that advice. The first time, I wasn't. Not even a little. Now, I believed I was. At the very least, I wanted to see where this thing between Emerson and me could go, as long as that was what she wanted too. "I am."

He typed something into his mobile and, seconds later, mine buzzed.

"That's her home address," he said, and then went back to looking at something on his screen. "You won't get there tonight, I'm afraid." He looked over at Brian. "And we aren't going to make it home either. Highway 95 is closed and so is 495."

"Cool!" Brian exclaimed. "We get to stay here overnight."

"Wish I felt your enthusiasm, but, yes, that appears to be the case."

"We're only a few minutes from Saint's apartment… scratch that…it's my apartment now."

Stephen stood and walked over to the restaurant's windows. "I'm thinking we should get our food to go. It's quite nasty out."

Brian nodded. "This is awesome."

Like Stephen, I wished I shared the boy's enthusiasm. Here I was, less than two hours from Emerson, and yet I couldn't get to her. My frustration and disappointment were palpable.

The waiter brought our to-go packages, and the three of us stood to don jackets, hats, and gloves. Fortunately, I'd thought to bring them after Rashid ran them out to his boyfriend.

My cousin rested his hand on my shoulder. "It's supposed to clear up by morning."

"Right," I muttered.

"Nora and the girls are spending the night in Newport. Too dangerous to be out on the roads," Stephen said, joining me in the kitchen. "Thanks for setting Brian up in the office. He won't get much sleep tonight."

I hadn't given him access to classified information or technology, but that didn't mean there weren't countless things he could explore on the computers Decker had set up in addition to what Saint had in his office when he lived in the apartment.

"Can I get you a drink?" I asked.

"Might as well. Not as if I'm going to be driving tonight, or getting called in to work the emergency room."

I poured us both a brandy and handed him a glass.

"Let's talk about tomorrow," he said, setting his drink down on the coffee table and leaning forward with his elbows on his knees.

Emerson

"It's okay, Mom, I really didn't expect you and Dad to come down tomorrow." I was watching the snow plow clear my street out of my kitchen window; I couldn't imagine how much harder it would be for them to plow in a city like Boston. Newport was tiny by comparison in both size and population.

"We'll make it up to you next week, sweetheart. Your dad and I are both so proud of you."

"It's just an associate professorship, Mom." She said something I couldn't understand. "You're breaking up."

"Sorry, honey, I had my hand over the phone. Your dad wants to talk to you."

"Hey, Emme…" I heard my dad say as a car pulled up in front of my building. It looked a lot like the Jaguar Tommy had told me he'd borrowed from Angel. In fact, it was the same one. I was sure of it. What was he doing back here?

"Emme?"

"Sorry, Dad. I need to call you back." I ended the call and watched as the two front doors and one in the back opened. I held my breath when I saw Stephen get out of the passenger side. My eyes filled with tears when I saw Lynx get out of the driver's side.

He looked up, and I raised my hand, not knowing if he could see me or not. I dropped my phone on the counter when he raised his in answer.

I pulled the sash of the robe that covered my flannel pajamas tighter and looked down at the bunny slippers I'd worn last night, mostly for Eleanor's and Elizabeth's sake. It wasn't the sexiest look, but I didn't have time to worry about that.

Racing down the hallway, I opened the door and stuck my head into the guest room. "Nora," I whispered, hoping I could wake her without doing the same with the twins.

She opened her eyes and sat up.

"Stephen is here," I whispered. "With Lynx."

"Oh my God." She threw the covers off and got out of bed. At least we were both equally unsexy looking since she'd borrowed one of my other pairs of flannel pj's. "We'll get the girls up and get out of here as fast as we can."

"No, I mean, don't feel like you have to hurry."

She smiled at me. "Right. We won't hurry. In fact, I think we'll hang out here with you all day. You won't mind that, right?"

I was about to tell her to shut up when I heard a knock at my door and froze.

"Go," Nora said, pushing me out of the doorway and toward the front door.

I wiped my sweaty hands on my pajama bottoms and took a deep breath, wishing I'd brushed my teeth again after I drank a cup of coffee. When I stopped walking, Nora gave me another push.

I put my hand on the doorknob and slowly turned it. I couldn't speak when I saw Lynx standing on the other side.

"Emerson," he said, opening it the rest of the way, pushing inside, and wrapping his arms around my waist. He leaned down and rested his forehead against mine. "Do you have any idea how happy I am to see you?"

"What are you doing here? Not that I'm not happy that you're here. It's just that I haven't heard from you since you left. I mean, I know about your brother, so I understand—"

At the same time Lynx grasped the back of my neck with his hands, his lips covered mine in a kiss.

I felt two people brush past us. If they said anything, I didn't hear it. All I could hear was the blood pumping in my body as my heart beat out of my chest.

Lynx's tongue thrust into my mouth and wound around mine. I tightened my grasp around his neck, never wanting to let go.

I lost track of time while Lynx pressed harder into our kiss, running his hands over my body. I gasped when he covered my breasts with his hands. I tried to break our kiss to look around for Nora and her family, but he brought one hand back to my neck and held me in place.

"Thanks for the ride," I heard Stephen say.

"Welcome," Lynx answered, briefly breaking our kiss only to dive right back in when we heard my front door open and then, several seconds later, close behind my friend, his cousin, and their family.

Lynx lifted me into his arms. "Bedroom?"

"That way," I said, pointing down the hall.

He stalked there, holding my body close to his and then set me on my feet.

When I started to untie the sash of my robe, he stopped me. "I'll do it," he growled.

Within seconds, I stood before him naked and watched as he removed his clothes. He pushed me onto the bed, shackling my hands above my head with one hand while he crushed my mouth with his.

I couldn't stop myself from bucking beneath him.

"Hold still," he said, covering my body with his and then dipping his head to my straining nipple. The sharp sting of his bite fed my arousal to the point where I thrashed beneath him. I could feel his steely erection slide between my slick folds. I wrapped my legs around his waist and locked my ankles.

Slowly, he eased into my wetness, only picking up his pace when he was in as far as he could go. He reared back and thrust in again, pounding into me in a rhythm I had come to crave.

He drove into me again and again with heavy grunts of exertion. I tightened my thighs as his shaft jerked against my body's small contractions, clutching his amazing cock.

"Yes, now, now…" I cried, my nails digging into the flesh of his back.

"Fucking, yes, Emerson. Now!" he demanded, surging into me harder, faster, deeper.

I felt myself coming apart beneath him, my orgasm only intensifying when I felt him come inside me. He wrapped his arm around the back of my knee, opening me wider as he continued to surge inside me.

"I can't get enough of you," he groaned. Just when I thought he'd stop and roll his body next to mine, he roared back with an unexpected urgency. *"Fuck,"* he cried out again, and I could feel him emptying still more inside me.

I started to move, but Lynx latched onto my butt, holding me against him.

"I'm not letting you go, Emerson. Not ever."

"I don't want you to."

He pulled back and looked into my eyes, his big hand still clenching my bottom. "I love you," he said, his green eyes piercing mine. "You're mine, now and forever."

"I love you too, Lynx."

"Say it again," he growled.

"I love you, Lynx."

"Now say the rest."

"I want you to fuck me senseless."

He smiled. "Not exactly what I was looking for, but I'll take it."

"I'm yours, Lynx, and you're mine. Now and forever."

—:—

"I should call Nora and apologize. I didn't even say goodbye. Or thank her," I said hours later when I rolled out of bed. Every inch, every muscle of my body ached from being sucked, laved, kneaded, fucked, but mainly and mostly—loved.

Instead of getting up to look for my phone, I watched Lynx pad his way to the bathroom, remembering how I'd ogled his ass the morning I passed him as he went into my building and I went out. It was so much better than with clothes covering it.

He turned around and smiled, holding his hand out to me. "Shower with me," he said, and I smiled back.

"I think we should take a bath instead." I led him down the hallway to the guest bath and pushed the door open. The claw-foot tub had been the main reason I'd rented the apartment, even though at the time, I wondered if I'd ever use it.

—:—

"How long can you stay?" I asked him as we sat at the dining room table and nibbled leftover Brazilian food Nora and I had brought back with us last night.

"About that…"

I raised my eyes and looked into his.

"There's something I'd like to discuss with you."

"Okay," I murmured, dreading whatever it was he was about to say.

"I'm leaving MI6."

"Oh."

He reached over and put his hand on mine. "I want you to know that I made the decision to do so several days ago."

I was almost afraid to breathe. What did this mean? I had no idea.

"I'm sure you're aware that my brother was injured during the op in which Saint and Dr. Benjamin were extracted."

"Yes."

"I don't know what details you've been made aware of…"

"None, really," I murmured.

"There was a chance he might not regain use of his right hand and arm."

I gasped, and he squeezed my fingers.

"He doesn't have full mobility yet, but he's very close, and while my leaving MI6 won't mean I'll avoid being in situations where my life might be threatened or I'll face certain danger, what I do know is that when I'm not working, I want to spend every moment possible with you, Emerson."

I kept my gaze focused on him but wasn't sure what to say.

He took a deep breath. "When I am working, I want the ability to choose what missions I'll accept." He scrubbed his face with his hand. "I wish you'd say something, my darling."

"I want to spend every moment with you too."

He smiled, and the tension around his eyes melted away. "I'm very happy to hear that."

"What will you do?"

"I've been extended an offer from the firm where Keon is a partner."

I'd just been offered an associate professorship, but at that moment, I realized that if I had to move to Texas to be with Lynx, I would. "Where will you live?" I asked.

"Wherever you do."

My eyes opened wide. "What do you mean?"

"Boston. Here. Cape Cod. Timbuktu. It doesn't matter where we live, Emerson. As long as we're together, that's all I care about."

"You said you were extended an offer…"

"I haven't given MI6 my final resignation yet."

"Why not?"

He cupped my cheek with his hand. "I had to talk to you first. Make sure you…"

I covered his hand with mine. "Make sure I…what?"

"Felt the same way about me as I feel about you."

"You know I do."

"Yes. I do."

"So what will you do now?"

Lynx stood so abruptly it startled me. He reached under me, and suddenly, I was in his arms. "I'm going to fuck you senseless," he said right before his mouth captured mine.

Epilogue

Lynx

Three Years Later

When I came out of the kitchen door and stood on the back porch, I could see my wife and her parents sitting on the sand. Our two-year-old son, Finn Arlo—his middle name, for my father—sat between his grandparents. Emerson held our one-year-old daughter, Charlie Annaliese—her middle name, for my mother—on her lap. From where I stood, I could see the baby rubbing her mum's belly, endlessly chattering at her brother or sister, who would arrive in the fall.

My cousin Stephen and his family were scheduled to arrive this afternoon, as was my brother. We might even see Saint, Angel, and Typhon before the Fourth of July holiday weekend was over.

I looked out at Cape Cod Bay and thought back to the summer when I imagined this could one day be my life, afraid to speak the words aloud even to myself, and now, here I was, my every dream realized.

My beautiful Emerson insisted she loved being pregnant as much as she loved being a mother. She still taught at the War College, but more and more, she gave up her lectures in Newport, and offered them online instead.

Last night, as we laid on the hanging daybed on the back porch, we agreed that our third child would be named for her father and brother regardless of whether the baby was a boy or a girl. The spelling would vary, as would the middle name. I'd made the offer when Finn was born, but my lovingly sensitive wife said she wasn't ready to bestow that particular name.

I'd learned straight away, when I was an undercover MI6 agent and she an international policy writer, that in most matters, my wife was far smarter and quite a bit more capable than I—with the exception of cooking, which I was happy to take on, particularly since I'd given up most missions in favor of becoming the U.S. Chief Operating Officer of the Invincible Intelligence and Security Group. Rile was my European counterpart, and Typhon was in charge of Asian operations.

We'd grown from the original four, plus me, to a total of twenty-five agents who operated all over the world.

I watched as Emerson handed baby Charlie to her grandmother and walked in my direction.

"Everything okay?" she asked, wrapping her arms around my waist. I kissed the top of her head, where the scar from her staples only showed when her hair was wet.

"Everything is perfect," I murmured, moving her hair so I could nip the soft skin on her neck.

"Are you sure you won't mind my parents keeping Finn and Charlie here with them next week?"

"Are you sure you won't mind?" I rested my hand on her belly, loving that being pregnant didn't stop her from wearing a bikini, or better yet, walk naked as often as privacy would allow.

"We need to find a bigger house," she said, tapping her lower lip with her fingertips.

We'd given up the apartment in Boston when we were pregnant with our first child. Two apartments, actually, since Rashid and David were fully ensconced in Emerson's.

We had a house in Newport, but our family was quickly outgrowing it. Next week, we would decide whether to sell it and buy a bigger place there or choose another city entirely. Honestly, I didn't care where we lived. All that mattered to me was that Emerson was happy.

"I should get Charlie," she said, watching as her parents stood to come up to the house. "She's probably hungry."

I checked the time. Finn was likely ready for a nap as well.

"I'd like to talk to the two of you for a minute," said Rick.

Rebecca handed Charlie to Emerson and took Finn's hand, leading him inside.

"Wait!" Emerson cried, and Finn came running back.

"Love you, Mum," he said in words that only my wife and I understood. When she knelt down, Finn put his arms around her and Charlie and gave them both a kiss.

"I bet your grandmum will read you a story if you ask nicely," she said before he ran back to Rebecca and put his tiny hand in hers. I couldn't imagine a better life for our children, and was thankful for the amount of time Emerson's parents spent with our family.

Emerson sat down at the patio table and got Charlie settled on her breast. It was a sight I would never tire of.

Rick motioned for me to take a seat before he did the same. He folded his hands and rested them on the table.

"Your mother and I have given this a lot of thought, and we've decided to downsize."

"What does that mean?" Emerson asked.

He pulled what looked like a real estate flier from his pocket, unfolded it, and handed it to his daughter.

"You're buying the house next door?" she gasped. "But…why?" Her eyes met mine, and I recognized her silent pleas.

"Rick," I began, but before I could say another word, he held up his hand.

"We want our grandchildren to be as close as possible, year-round, and I can't think of a better place to grow up than on the bay."

"You want us to buy this house?" she asked him, but then looked at me. "Can we afford it? I mean, I know we can afford it, but, Dad, you're kind of putting us on the spot. We need to talk this over, and—"

"Emme, the house is already yours. Yours and Lynx's if you both want it. Your mother and I signed the quitclaim deed this morning." He pushed his chair back and stood. "I'll give you two some time to talk it over."

"What do you think?" she murmured.

"It's where our life together truly began."

"I never dreamed this would be our life."

I leaned over and kissed my beloved daughter's tiny hand, and then kissed my beloved wife. "I did."

Keep reading for
a sneak peek at
Edged
a book in
Heather Slade's
Invincibles Team One Series

1

Edge

I had three more nights in Texas, and then I had to fly to Boston—a place I had zero interest in going, for a reason I didn't give a shit about.

If it were for work, that would be different. If there was a mission to be had, I was the first to raise my hand, more so now that I'd left the rules and regulations of MI5 behind and was a partner in the Invincible Intelligence and Security Group.

A partner's wife had first called us the Invincibles, and it took. Yeah, it sounded cocky as shit, but we all were, so what the hell?

I'd tried to get my best friend, Miles "Grinder" Stone, to come out with me tonight, but he was in what I referred to as his dark place.

The man had PTSD from a deployment with ISAF— the International Security Assistance Force—a NATO-led security mission in Afghanistan. I admired the guy enough to respect the times when he wasn't interested in socializing.

I could've invited Cortez "Rile" DeLéon, the eldest of the four partners, but that would be almost as bad as going out with my secondary school headmaster.

It wasn't as though I wouldn't know anyone at the Long Branch tonight or any other night. Most of the hands who worked on the King-Alexander Ranch, where I lived, frequented the place.

I pulled into the parking lot, surprised at how few cars were in it, and found a spot not too far from the entrance.

Climbing out of the 1957 Ford ranch pickup I'd borrowed, I slammed the creaky door closed. The locks had a tendency to stick, so I didn't bother trying to secure it. If any wanker tried to make off with it, this truck, like the rest of those at the ranch, was equipped with a tracking device that would allow the engine to be shut off remotely.

I hadn't done it yet, but if I was ever given the chance to, I'd press the kill button as soon as the driver hit a decent speed. For the Ford, that would be about seventy since the old thing wouldn't go much faster. I chuckled, thinking about the look on the bastard's face when the truck flipped end to end on one of the area's dirt roads.

It was hotter than Hades tonight with close to one hundred percent humidity, but I still wore my pearl snap shirt and pressed Cinch jeans. Anything else would get me tossed out of the Branch—as we affectionately called it—on my arse.

Walking past a newer edition pickup, I averted my eyes when I saw the front bench seat was occupied by a couple shagging. I was almost to the back bumper when I realized the sounds the woman was making weren't those of pleasure.

I spun around, wrenched open the door, grabbed the asshole by the shirt collar, and pulled him away from the woman I now could tell was trying to fight the guy off.

"What the fuck?" the guy slurred.

I threw him up against the truck next to his, and as I did, I got a whiff of alcohol.

Holding the drunk by the neck, I turned around to tell the woman to get dressed and get the hell out of there, but she was ahead of me. Instead of getting out of the passenger side, she climbed out the driver's side, walked straight over to the wanker, and slammed her knee into his crotch. I cringed thinking about how much that had to hurt.

When she threw a punch into the guy's gut, I thought I may have fallen in love at first sight.

I heard a car pull up and looked over my shoulder, surprised to see the sheriff. "Hey, Mac. Good timing."

"What's goin' on here?"

"The fucker tried to rape me," said the woman, wiping what looked like blood from a cut on her face.

I still had the guy by the back of the collar. I let him go, and he fell to the ground, hands on his crotch.

"I got this, Edge. You go on and get outta here."

"Thanks, mate. I owe you one." In my line of work, the last thing I could afford was to be a witness in a rape trial.

I walked over to the old Ford and was about to climb in when I heard a soft voice ask me to wait. When I turned around, the feisty woman who slammed her would-be rapist in the balls with her knee, got on her tiptoes and planted a kiss right on my lips. It wasn't a chaste one either. "Thanks, Edge," she said as she walked away.

I shook my head and climbed into the truck, wishing I could stay, but knowing I couldn't.

Two nights later, wanting to grab a pint before I left town for God knew how long, I went back to the Branch. It was harder to find a place to park tonight; it looked like the place was packed.

I pulled open the heavy door and made my way through the crowd. When I got up to the bar, the owner brought me a beer before I had a chance to order.

"This one's on her." He pointed to the end of the bar.

I looked to where he motioned and met the woman's eyes. "What's her name?"

"That's Rebel."

About the Author

USA Today and Amazon Top 15 Bestselling Author Heather Slade writes shamelessly sexy, edge-of-your seat romantic suspense.

She gave herself the gift of writing a book for her own birthday one year. Fifty-plus books later (and counting), she's having the time of her life.

The women Slade writes are self-confident, strong, with wills of their own, and hearts as big as the Colorado sky. The men are sublimely sexy, seductive alphas who rise to the challenge of capturing the sweet soul of a woman whose heart they'll hold in the palm of their hand forever. Add in a couple of neck-snapping twists and turns, a page-turning mystery, and a swoon-worthy HEA, and you'll be holding one of her books in your hands.

She loves to hear from my readers. You can contact her at heather@heatherslade.com

To keep up with her latest news and releases, please visit her website at www.heatherslade.com to sign up for her newsletter.

MORE FROM AUTHOR HEATHER SLADE

BUTLER RANCH
Kade's Worth
Brodie's Promise
Maddox's Truce
Naughton's Secret
Mercer's Vow
Kade's Return
Butler Ranch Christmas

**WICKED WINEMAKERS
FIRST LABEL**
Brix's Bid
Ridge's Release
Press' Passion
Zin's Sins
Tryst's Temptation

**WICKED WINEMAKERS
SECOND LABEL**
Beau's Beloved
Coming Soon:
Cru's Crush
Bones' Bliss
Snapper's Seduction
Kick's Kiss

ROARING FORK RANCH
Coming Soon:
Roaring Fork Wrangler
Roaring Fork Roughstock
Roaring Fork Rockstar
Roaring Fork Rooker
Roaring Fork Bridger

**THE ROYAL AGENTS
OF MI6**
Make Me Shiver
Drive Me Wilder
Feel My Pinch
Chase My Shadow
Find My Angel

**K19 SECURITY
SOLUTIONS TEAM ONE**
Razor's Edge
Gunner's Redemption
Mistletoe's Magic
Mantis' Desire
Dutch's Salvation

**K19 SECURITY
SOLUTIONS TEAM TWO**
Striker's Choice
Monk's Fire
Halo's Oath
Tackle's Honor
Onyx's Awakening

**K19 SHADOW OPERATIONS
TEAM ONE**
Code Name: Ranger
Code Name: Diesel
Code Name: Wasp
Code Name: Cowboy
Code Name: Mayhem

**K19 ALLIED INTELLIGENCE
TEAM ONE**
Code Name: Ares
Code Name: Cayman
Code Name: Poseidon
Coming soon:
Code Name: Zeppelin
Code Name: Magnet

**K19 ALLIED INTELLIGENCE
TEAM TWO**
Coming Soon:
Code Name: Michelangelo
Code Name: Typhon
Code Name: Hornet
Code Name: Reaper
Code Name: Rogue

**PROTECTORS
UNDERCOVER**
Undercover Agent
Coming Soon:
Undercover Savior
Undercover Prince
Undercover Infidel
Undercover Assassin

**THE INVINCIBLES
TEAM ONE**
Decked
Edged
Grinded
Riled
Smoked

**THE INVINCIBLES
TEAM TWO**
Bucked
Irished
Sainted
Hammered
Ripped

**THE UNSTOPPABLES
TEAM ONE**
Furied
Merried

**COWBOYS OF
CRESTED BUTTE**
A Cowboy Falls
A Cowboy's Dance
A Cowboy's Kiss
A Cowboy Stays
A Cowboy Wins